BOOKS BY RICHARD TORONTO

War Over Lemuria (2013)
Shaverology - A Shaver Mystery Home Companion (2013)
Shavertron – The Mimeograph Years (2013)
Shavertron – The MacPlus Years (2014)
Shavertron – The Lettershop Years (2014)
Shavertron – The Mimeograph Years (2014)
Rokfogo – The Mysterious Pre-Deluge Art of
Richard S. Shaver, vols. 1 & 2 (2014)
Hollywood and Vain – A Frisco Detective Mystery (2025)
(published in 2020 as Cold War Hot Lead under pseud-
onym Mace Palmer)
Half Past Satan – (2025) (published in 2022 as
The Mind Fuhrer under pseudonym Mace Palmer)
Doom Town and the Atomic Blonde from Sector 9 (2026)

ATOMIC
CRIME
LIBRARY

NUDIST CAMP
CONFIDENTIAL

A
FRISCO DETECTIVE MYSTERY

RICHARD TORONTO

SAN FRANCISCO

ATOMIC CRIME LIBRARY

CHAPTER ONE

was standing in a parking lot off the 101 near Solvang, digging through my purse for the keys to my Rambler rail top convertible when two bozos in lederhosen strong-armed me. Yes, you heard me, *lederhosen* — those crazy embroidered short pants with suspenders? In a flash the Krauts had me surrounded, and it was pretty clear they weren't looking for a donation to the Oktoberfest fund. One of them grabbed me from behind while the other aimed a Government Colt .45 automatic at my dainty midsection. A single pill from that artillery piece would make me an organ donor as far away as Catalina.

The creep who had me in his clutches wore a Tyrolean hat with a red feather. He had a square jaw, clodhopper shoes, thick, wool socks that crawled up to his kneecaps, and an all around mean look. His pallid complexion had the texture of peeled, dried apple, but he had muscles. I could feel his biceps tense around my ample chest.

The joker in front of me was a dead ringer for the other one, only bigger. As Confucius used to say: "All Occidentals look alike," and the goofy outfits these white boys wore made them look straight off the assembly line.

The hambo with the gat gripped it like a gorilla with a ripe banana. His nose bent slightly to the left. How it got that way was anybody's guess. A V-shaped nick etched the top of his right ear, and his teeth were a nasty shade of nicotine. He showed them to me, lifting his upper lip in a greasy snarl. He must have thought I would

Paloma Liu Tsong

It said I'd won a two week vacation, all expenses paid.

melt with fear, and go along with whatever they had in mind.

Not that I'm complaining. I'd had a fantastic day before these two showed up. I'd been cruising down El Camino Real with the top down, enjoying every mile of the California countryside. Birds were singing, the central coast sun was shining, and I'd hit every green light between Pismo Beach and Solvang, which is where I'd just had lunch at the Twin Cars Diner.

Even better, I was on an all expenses paid vacation, sans my partner and fellow private dick, Alexander "Buster" Blade. He was on vacation too — at San Francisco General Hospital. His broken leg was in traction, hanging from the ceiling of Room 217, poor guy.

His untimely accident put me in charge of Confidential Investigations, our San Francisco detective agency, where I whiled away the hours reading *Cosmopolitan* and hoping a client would magically appear. Two weeks later, I'd read every magazine on the Chinese newsstand at Grant Avenue and Washington and still no client. It got so bad I thought someone had taped a QUARANTINE sign on the door. Life was absolute dullsville, until 10 o'clock Monday morning when the mailman delivered the mail.

Although the mailman wasn't exactly a client, he brought something almost as good: a letter addressed to me, personally. The return address intrigued me — Sunland Vacation Camp, P.O. Box 23, Tujunga, California.

"Dear Miss Liu Tsong," the letter began. "Congratulations! You are one of our three lucky winners — chosen by random drawing — of a two-week vacation at Sunland Vacation Camp in beautiful Southern California! Please register at our Sunland Lodge no later than 8 PM August 14, 1951 to claim your prize."

Strange that I couldn't remember entering this contest, but I had only five days to register or I'd lose my prize. There was more: "Don't forget to bring plenty of suntan oil! Signed, Laura Borealis, Camp Administrator."

Miss Borealis enclosed a full-color brochure lauding the benefits of Sunland Vacation Camp. The photos showed a swimming pool, quaint looking guest cottages, a volleyball court, and expansive, well-trimmed lawns surrounded by majestic pines. There was even a cascading waterfall.

I was sold! Not only had I never won a contest, but I had never even had what you'd call a vacation. My life was ticking away in an empty office. So, I turned out the lights, locked the door, and taped a sign on the glass: "BACK IN TWO WEEKS." Yes, it was my lucky day.

From the Mayfair Building on Bush I walked to my Chinatown apartment on Clay to pack my things. Two hours later, I'd stowed my luggage in the Rambler and was ready to go. First, I drove to San Francisco General to inform Alex of my good fortune. I knew he'd be thrilled to hear about my prize.

"Are you kidding me? A vacation? What about the office? What about the clients who need us?"

"What clients, Alex?" I fumed. "I've been twiddling my thumbs in that office for weeks! Other than the mailman and a hooker who asked to use the restroom, no one has set foot in there but me. I won this contest and I'm going to take it! I'll only be gone two weeks, tops. And it's a vacation camp. Nothing to do but swim, breath fresh air, gaze at the clouds, and before you know it, I'll be back at work full of energy."

"I see," he pouted, trying a new approach. "You've already made up your mind. Okay, go ahead. Take a vacation while I lay here, unable to earn a living and pay the bills; send me a postcard if you find the time. I'll see you when you get back. If it isn't too much trouble, call me when you've checked in; if they have telephones there."

How pathetic can you get? I didn't give him a chance to think of a new reason why I shouldn't go. So, I puckered up, smacked him on the forehead, and slipped out the door. With that unpleasant business out of the way, I drove my two-tone green and ivory Rambler to the 101 Highway — El Camino Real — heading south.

Everything was jake until the two Krauts in short pants rained on my parade. I think that was where I left off. Yes, in the parking lot of the Twin Cars Diner. So, when the punk holding me from behind decided to clamp his right arm around my neck, I took charge.

I widened my stance and moved my hips to one side. That partially freed me from the palooka's grasp. Before he could yodel the German national anthem, I whipped around to face him in an offensive position. I grabbed his arm, slipped my right leg behind his, gave him my hip and

A few quick moves of the White Crane and he was airborne.

threw him over. He was airborne before landing head first on top of the guy with the gat. That's when the gat went off, blowing a hole in the dirt parking lot. For a moment my blitzkrieg dazed them. They just sat on the ground with their mouths open.

What they failed to realize was, you can't be an exotic dancer in Chinatown like I was without picking up a few useful skills, and I learned plenty. Like the way of the White Crane, taught by Fang Qiniang in old China. It came in handy at Andy Wong's Sky Room, where I got my fair share of unwanted advances, especially after my late night shows. Whenever a rowdy sailor boy refused to get the message, a few quick moves of the White Crane had him counting stars he'd never seen before.

The gunshot brought out a flood of diners into the parking lot. I was ready for my next round with the gunsels, until they had second thoughts. They sprang up, hightailed it to their jalopy, and vamoosed. For three whole seconds I thought about chasing them. Then I remembered I was on vacation! Besides, my little Rambler never would have caught their beefy DeSoto V-8 Firedome.

A man in a starched white shirt and trousers creased like knife blades rushed up to me. He belonged to the Wonder Bread delivery truck parked next to my car, and he looked worried.

"Are you all right, Miss? Did they hurt you?"

"Thank you, no. They were amateurs."

"I gotta say, you sure made short work of those two. Are you ex-military?"

"Ex fan dancer," I replied. "Andy Wong's Sky Room, Frisco. You'd be surprised what you learn in Chinatown. Thanks for checking on me, but I'd better be going. I've got to reach Tujunga before dark."

"You should get there in plenty of time, Miss. Be safe!"

CHAPTER TWO

l Camino Real cuts through a cleft of solid rock at the narrow Gaviota Pass. The towering granite walls of the pass flipped a switch in my brain that sent me right back into vacation mode. Up to now, I couldn't get those two lederhosen-wearing palookas off my mind. What were they up to? Maybe it was just strong-arm robbery, but what was with the lederhosen? There had to be something more going on, and the thought bothered me. I emerged from Gaviota Pass to the vast Pacific Ocean on my right. It looked bluer than it did back in Frisco.

In a way, I was returning to my Spanish heritage. When I was a kid my mother told me stories about our family's Spanish land grant near Santa Barbara. When the Americans invaded Alta California in 1846, they took our rancho and carved it up into parcels to sell to Anglo settlers. Having lost everything, our family relocated throughout the territory. My immediate family settled in the Sacramento River delta, an agricultural wonderland. But Southern California was where it all began.

I had a lot of catching up to do, things to see. San Francisco and the tiny delta town I hailed from were all I had ever known. There, I'm known as Liu Tsong, a Chinese girl and "exotic" dancer in the Chinatown club scene. But those days are over. Six months ago I got my private investigator's license and turned in my ostrich fans. Being half Chinese, there's an unwritten San Francisco law that says I belong in Chinatown. That's just the way it is. But in Southern California I will be Paloma, a Spanish Californio who looks just a little different. Embracing my Latin side will be something new for me.

From Gaviota Beach I drove the coastline all the way to Ventura. I made mental notes of beaches I passed along the way: Refugio, Arroyo Quemada, El Capitan. Several miles later I lost count as the palm trees blazed across the azure blue backdrop of the Pacific. I drove with the top down, and it was pure heaven.

I pulled into a Flying A service station in Santa Barbara to gas up. I'd brought a picnic basket with a light meal, so after the attendant washed my windshield, checked my tire pressure and oil level, I drove to East Beach on Cabrillo, edging into a parking space under a row of slender palm trees. The beach lay just beyond the trees, so, picnic basket in hand, I headed out. I spread a blanket on the white sand and ate my lunch, watching the waves come and go. The Channel Islands shimmered like phantom schooners on the horizon. An hour later, I was back on the 101, driving through Summerland, La Conchita, and Oil Piers Beach, until turning inland onto Highway 33 at Ventura.

There, the cool coastal landscape suddenly changed to dry heat. I pulled over at Mission Buenaventura to raise my convertible top against the sun. From the 33, I took the 118 and followed road signs to San Fernando, where I stopped at Mission San Fernando Rey de España to buy postcards. I had learned that sending postcards is what you do when you're on vacation. Having never had one, I read about the postcard rule in a *Saturday Evening Post*. I thought I should stick with tradition.

From photos I'd seen, none of these old missions looked alike. This one had arches and columns cascading down a long corridor that faced the road. I parked the Rambler and followed a sign with a pointing finger that said: "Gift Shop." Like all California missions, the gift shop is the entrance to the rooms and gardens inside. You pay the clerk, get a brochure, and explore. But I had no time for the self-guided tour.

The postcard rack had views of all the missions. I bought a card with a stoic-looking padre in a brown robe standing next to a Moorish style fountain, and another with an aerial shot of the San Fernando Valley. The third was a joke card of an old mission well. Someone's feet were sticking out of the well. "Wish You Were Here," it read. Alex will get that one as soon as I get settled at camp. The wagon wheel clock on the gift shop wall said it was nearly five o'clock, and I still had mountain roads to travel. I paid the clerk and was on my way.

Little Tujunga Canyon Road took me up the mountain, where it forked at Big Oak Road, no more than a wagon trail strewn with potholes. The Rambler bumped along like a flea with a hotfoot. My contest letter said to watch for an iron gate next to a tall madrone. The gate would have a sign on it — "Sound Horn. Gatekeeper will come to meet you." I guess they don't like uninvited guests at Sunland Vacation Camp.

The tree was an easy landmark, the tallest madrone on the road. As described, the iron gate was there, too, with the sign instructing me to honk my horn. I honked. Five minutes went by. The silence was deafening, and I was wasting valuable vacation time. I honked again. A distant figure appeared at the far end of the road. As the figure came closer, I made out his features. He appeared to be in his mid 60s, with

Gatekeeper

a full, white beard, bib overalls, long-sleeved shirt, and sea captain's hat. In time he reached the gate.

"Got an invitation, Miss?" he asked in a voice like truck tires on a gravel road.

I got out of the car, handed my letter over the gate.

"Oh, you're one of our contest winners!" he bellowed. "The other two are already here. Welcome to Sunland, Miss."

At that, Gatekeeper pulled a large, silver key ring from his overalls and inserted a key into the padlock, removing the heavy chain that kept unwanted guests at bay. He beckoned me to drive forward. Once I was inside, he replaced the chain and padlock.

"Just follow me, Miss," he grated.

I wasn't sure why I had to follow him. I saw only one road ahead of us, with no turnoffs on either side. But, I obeyed nonetheless, moving at a snail's pace behind his steady gait.

We meandered uphill about a quarter mile before the camp featured in my brochure came into view. I saw rustic cabins randomly built on a sloping hill. The spacious lawns were there, too, with larger buildings in the distance, but no camp guests.

"Where is everyone?"

"Dance in the Rec Hall tonight, Miss," he replied. "But here's where you'll want to go."

Gatekeeper gestured to a small parking area in front of a log chalet. The carved wood sign above the front porch read: "Sunland Lodge." I parked my car and rolled the window down as Gatekeeper came up alongside me.

"This is where you'll check in, Miss," he said. "Miss Laura's expecting you."

At that, the codger meandered off toward a large building in the distance.

It felt good to stretch my legs after the tense drive up the mountain road. Sunset was an hour ago, and light was fading. Stars seemed brighter and the sky darker here on the mountain. It was nothing like back home.

As I climbed the wide staircase, I noticed the lodge walls were made of heavy logs, stacked one on top of the other. The spaces between were filled with adobe. The lobby looked as rustic as the outside. Everything seemed to have tree bark on it. Deer antlers decorated the walls on either side of a massive stone fireplace made of river rock. No fire today, though. It was warm outside, even at this hour.

The polished redwood front desk had a round metal gong within easy reach. A hand carved wood sign said: "Hit gong for assistance." Another sign, this one above the office door, read: "He who seeks Nakedness, seeks the Truth, he who fears the Truth, fears Nakedness." I picked up the hammer and struck the gong.

"That's a curious proverb for a vacation camp," I thought. As I waited, I looked around the room.

Framed photographs of happy Sunland vacationers adorned a wall near the front desk. They were playing volleyball, swimming in a lake, and sunning themselves in lounge chairs next to the swimming pool. They all had one thing in common — the people were all stark naked! There were family photos, too — mom, dad, the kids — all naked as jaybirds. That's odd, I thought. What kind of camp is this? I picked up the padded hammer and struck the gong again, with results this time.

A woman in her mid-50s emerged from the office: blue eyes, brown hair streaked with gray, slightly overweight, with a smile on her tanned, pleasant face. There were more intimate details about her I could share, but won't, because like the subjects in the photographs, she was stark naked too.

"Welcome! You must be Miss Paloma!" the woman enthused. "You're our third and final contest winner to arrive this week! I'm Laura. I'm sure you'll enjoy your stay with us."

The blank stare on my face put a stop to her intake spiel.

"Ah, you're surprised, I can see that," she said. "Did I forget to mention that Sunland is a nudist camp?"

"I'm afraid so, Miss Borealis," I replied.

"I am so sorry. This must be something of a surprise for you. Oh, dear. But please, call me Miss Laura; we're very informal here. Besides, our guests use only their first names while staying at Sunland. Why, you ask? Because people in the outside textile world have

Laura Borealis

twisted views about nudism, I'm afraid. If word got out that some of our guests spent their summers at Sunland, in the nude, with others also in the nude, well, it could mean losing their jobs."

With no encouragement from me, she continued.

"To listen to the tabloids you'd think nudists are a bunch of oversexed swingers. I can assure you, Miss Paloma, it's just the opposite. Nudists are everyday people, wives and husbands, children and grandparents, who are, you might say, non-conformists by society's standards. They follow their own drummer. They're also curious individuals, willing to try alternative lifestyles. Sunland gives them a chance to live as nature intended, in a social, non-sexual setting. We have strict rules here, and everyone must agree to them or out they go. Number one on the list is, no ogling. Yes, that's a cardinal rule. We keep a close watch for COGs and lookie-loo's."

"COGs?"

"Creepy Old Guys," she replied. "If we catch anyone leering or staring at their fellow nudists, out they go."

"Well, that's good to know," I said for no particular reason. "I guess I didn't need to bring so many clothes." Her one-track mind didn't get my joke.

"Prurient sexual thoughts are non-existent at a nudist camp," Borealis prattled, "though the textile world seems to think otherwise. It's when you put on clothing that the uninvited stares, the lurid thoughts, and unwanted advances begin."

"I'm well acquainted with all of the above," I said.

I had the feeling nudist culture might frown on burlesque queens, so I kept my mouth shut, and it seemed Borealis was just getting warmed up.

"Well, don't you worry about that, Miss Paloma! That kind of behavior is not tolerated here! Our three cardinal rules are: no staring, no kissing or suggestive touching in public, and always put a clean towel on your chair. Within a week I'll wager you'll find nudist life more liberating than you ever imagined. It's all about positive body image. You'll find all body types here — as you can see by yours truly — and all ages, from grandparents to grandkids."

"Just one question," I interrupted. "Why did you wait until now to explain all this to me? There wasn't even a hint in my letter I'd be vacationing at a nudist colony."

Her expression melted like a pat of butter on a baked potato.

"I know, I know, and I'm ashamed of myself for leaving that out. Let me be frank, Miss Paloma. I wasn't sure you'd come if you knew Sunland was a nudist camp. The fact is, I want to hire you, and I don't want anyone to know you're a professional detective. And the only way you can go about your business here unnoticed would be as a fellow nudist."

"I see. My next question is, why me? There are plenty of private detectives in Los Angeles. Why bring me all the way from San Francisco?"

"Because I wanted someone from outside Los Angeles, to be as discrete and confidential as possible. You are an unfamiliar face here. More to the point, I'd prefer a female detective. A woman would see things differently than, well, a hard drinking, cigarette smoking, philandering male detective. You know how they are."

"Off the top of my head I can think of one. So, you say I'm to mingle with the other guests while I — what exactly is it you want me to do?"

"My goodness, would you look at the time! It's getting late, and you still have to settle into your cabin before lights out. We'll continue our discussion tomorrow, if that's all right with you? Meet me here at 10 o'clock tomorrow morning and we'll talk this over in private. Just remember, while you're here you must follow the same rules as any other Sunland guest. As far as anyone knows, you're simply one of our contest winners.

"We have a structured daily routine here, but you'll still have plenty of 'me' time. We serve breakfast between seven and nine AM, lunch from noon to one-thirty, dinner from six to seven-thirty. Everyone is expected to be in their cabins by 10 o'clock, and lights out at 11. The rest of the day is yours. Now, let me introduce you to one of our camp counselors. He'll give you our Sunland orientation."

Dick Barnett

At that, Borealis reached for a microphone under the counter and flicked a switch. "Counselor Dick, calling Counselor Dick! Please report to the lodge ASAP. Thank you." She turned off the microphone and resumed her talk.

"Dick is one of our oldest members," she explained. "By that I don't mean he's old. It's just that he's been spending the summer with us since he was a teen. He knows Sunland like the back of his hand. I'm sure you'll like him. While you're waiting, why not take a look around the lobby? You'll find our public phone booths are here, and we have a television set too, for those who enjoy that sort of thing. Viewing hours are between seven and ten every evening. Vending machines dispense healthy snacks if you're still hungry after meal times. There's something about that TV set that makes people crave snacks, I'm afraid."

While waiting for my camp counselor, I wandered over to the phone booths, looked at the TV set, and even studied the moose head on the wall. Then, Counselor Dick strode through the front door. He crossed the lobby and came to a stop right in front of me, all six feet, three inches of him, smiling broadly. And, like Miss Laura, he was completely nude from his manicured toenails to his sandy brown hair. His blue eyes, broad shoulders, lean, muscled torso, and luscious thighs gave him the look of an Olympic swimmer. He exuded an animal magnetism straight out of, 'Me Tarzan, You Jane.' That's when a fuse blew in my head.

I gurgled, "I like, yes."

Speaking to the marbled Adonis before me, Miss Laura said, "Dick, this is Miss Paloma. Give her the contest winner red carpet treatment, won't you? Oh, FYI; this is her first nudist camp experience."

"Hello, Paloma," the chiseled Greek god crooned like a sensuous cello. "Let's get you settled in. Okay with you?"

"Okay with me, yes I'm sure." I felt as goofy as a prom night wallflower.

CHAPTER THREE

L ike a lovesick rat, I followed my naked Pied Piper through the wide lodge doors to my Rambler parked out front. He wasn't easy to keep up with. He had a longer stride than mine, and was more self-assured in the dark. All I knew for sure was that Dick was my teacher and I was his student, ergo, this vacation was off to a great start.

"There's a parking space in front of your cabin," Dick said as he slid into the Rambler on the passenger side. I got in, turned the key, and ground first gear like my first day of Driver's Ed.

Dick pretended not to notice. "Just follow the road up this hill," he said, pointing through the windshield. "It leads straight to the cabins. They don't have numbers; they're named after birds. Yours is Jaybird. Mine is Owl, next door to yours. Looks like we're neighbors, Paloma."

Oh, my, garsh. How much better can this get, I wondered.

The Rambler bounced along a short distance of gravel road as I tried to get used to a naked man sitting so close to me on the front seat. Maybe the prickly sensations I felt on my nerve endings came from the thought that I was clothed and he wasn't. This was just the opposite of what I was used to in burlesque.

Jaybird was a quaint cabin made of split logs. It had a covered front porch with an antique rocking chair out front. The other cottages looked identical to mine except for the shutters. Jaybird's were green with jaybirds painted on them. Dick's had red shutters with owls. The other cabins had all sorts of other birds, and each had a car parked out front. I parked mine like the others, facing away from the cabin.

"This is it!" Dick chirped. "This is your new home away from home. I'll get your bags."

"Oh, don't worry about that, I can..."

"No, no, allow me!" Dick protested. "You're on vacation, and a prize winner besides. I'm here to take care of you."

Oh, how I wish you would, I thought. Dick opened the trunk and pulled out two suitcases. He turned to carry them into the cabin when I pointed to the Rambler's rear seat.

"I'm sorry, Dick," I said, "There's more in the back seat. I guess I over-packed."

"Nothing to be sorry about, Paloma, not when you're on vacation, I — wow! You sure did!" Dick yelped. "No matter, I've got 'em!"

Dick bent down to keep from hitting his head on the convertible top. Now, I know Miss Laura said staring was strictly off limits. But from where I stood, that rule just begged to be broken. I gave Dick's backside the sly once over. I've had my share of compliments on my own well-developed rear shanks, but if it were up to me, I'd have Dick's luscious hindquarters chiseled into the side of Mt. Rushmore.

He put one suitcase under his left arm, a second in his left hand, then picked up a third and fourth, springing up the garden path like my luggage was full of soap bubbles, which it wasn't.

"Would you mind opening the door, Paloma?" he asked sweetly. "It's unlocked. You'll find your key on the sitting room table over there, but no one locks their doors at Sunland. No need to."

We entered a cozy room, woodsy and old-fashioned. The furnishings were a Maxfield Parrish print of naked people frolicking by a lake, an end table and easy chair, a floor lamp with a mica shade, lace curtains on the windows — it was straight out of Tom Sawyer, except for the Sears Silvertone radio perched on a wall shelf.

"If it's okay with you, I'll put your bags in the bedroom," Dick said. "The bathroom is next to your bedroom. We're standing in the living room. There's no kitchen, since there's no need to cook, but there's a hotplate to heat water for tea. All meals are served in the Mess Hall. It's got a fully equipped commercial kitchen. Just show up at the right time and you'll be served. All meals are vegetarian to complement Sunland's healthy lifestyle."

I knew words were coming out of Dick's mouth, but he might as well have been speaking Swahili. I was still feasting my eyes on six foot three inches of Counselor Dick. I nodded my head up and down as he spoke, as if I understood every word. And he had plenty to say.

"You'll find the library next to the Mess Hall," he continued. "Besides soaking up rays and breathing in the fresh mountain air, we encourage guests to use the sport facilities. There's an outdoor tennis court with lights for night matches, a volleyball court, swimming pool, a lake with a sailboat — there's a sign-up sheet for the sailboat — and a Rec Hall where we hold Saturday night dances. Thursday is movie night. That begins at eight o'clock. They may not be first run, but they're entertaining. There's even a miniature golf course. The kids love that, but so do their parents."

Dick walked to the shelf with the radio and removed a book.

"Here's something for bedtime reading if you can't get to sleep right away. It'll answer any questions you might have about the nudist lifestyle."

"Sounds like I'll be pretty busy," I gargled. "Guess I'll leave my luggage stacked in the corner, now that I don't need clothing."

"That's right!" Dick enthused. "Clothing is not an option at a nudist camp. However, we do have a special robe for newbies like yourself. Some first timers are a tad shy about being naked in public for the first time. There's a robe in the closet if you feel the need for it."

"I think I'll be fine," I said. "Next time you see me, I'll be naked as a jaybird. Ha ha."

That amused him. His smile just about melted the clothes right off me. My face felt so hot I knew I was blushing. That should have been impossible for a gal like me: an exotic dancer on the strip club circuit — well, *former* exotic dancer.

Dick must have noticed my rosy glow, because he quickly wrapped up his spiel: "Okay then, I'd better be going so you can settle in," he said as he opened the door. "Besides, it's almost lights out. 'G'night, Paloma." The return spring on the screen door closed with a bang and he was gone.

I decided to unpack a few of my clothes anyway. I put them in the oak dresser next to my twin bed. I'll never know why I bothered, but it kept me busy. I pulled out my pink see-through nightgown that would have looked great on me. I shoved it into the drawer. I was a nudist 24/7 now; that meant at bedtime, too. No sexy chiffon lingerie for me. According to Miss Laura, it leads to lascivious thoughts.

I unpacked my toiletries and arranged them in the tiny bathroom. My bedroom had two twin beds, neatly made up with the blankets tucked super tight like in the Army. It seemed as though Sunland catered to married couples and families mostly, but also the occasional single like me, or Dick, for that matter. I stepped out of my summer dress, revealing the underpinnings of my textile incarceration. I unsnapped my nylons and rolled them off, wiggled out of my panty girdle, took off my bra, and, naked at last, slid under the sheets with my nudist manifesto, *There's More to Nudism Than Being Naked*. I was on my way to real freedom. From what, I wasn't sure, so I began reading.

"One of the major forces to a more rational, healthier attitude toward our bodies is the nudist movement," the author began. "Even newcomers to our nation's nudist parks find they are suddenly without the anatomical curiosity that is almost inescapable everywhere else.

"There is a billion dollar industry built around a driving curiosity about the human body. Burlesque, strip tease, stags, pornographic magazines, movies, and literature rake in a fabulous harvest, an unwholesome business that will die on the vine when the nudist park becomes as popular as the golf course. People will still admire a pretty girl, but she will be admired for her beauty and not for her significant curves."

I was already feeling guilty. Just six months ago, I was a willing participant in the burlesque industry the nudist movement wants to stamp out. Maybe Sunland offers a support group for former burlesque queens. "Hi, everyone. My name is Paloma and I'm a fan dancer." Now, as a professional investigator, the thought depressed me.

"Secondly," the author went on, "there is an immense freedom experienced in living entirely naked that is destroyed when garments are worn for concealment. A pair of sandals and a pair of sunglasses is all that is needed in sunny weather. The tiny bits of clothing considered 'essential' to a skimpy bathing suit are regarded in nudist society as unspeakably vulgar.

"Such swatches focus attention on certain areas of the body which in nudist parks are taken for granted. Nudists don't wear something for the sake of concealment, for they know to do so would make them objects of scrutiny."

The chiming of a distant bell interrupted my nudist education. Somewhere during Dick's whirlwind orientation he mentioned the lights out bell. I snapped off the reading lamp above my head and drifted off to sleep, naked as a jaybird.

CHAPTER FOUR

I was dreaming I was back in San Francisco, driving down steep California Street, when the brakes on my car gave out. Just before I crashed into the Ferry Building, I heard a distant clanging, like one of those metal triangles ranchers use to call in the hired hands. I was too sleepy to remember what it meant until my screen door squeaked open and slammed shut.

When I opened my eyes, I saw a hunk of naked beefcake gazing down at me. From my vantage point in bed, every inch of Counselor Dick was perfection. He let me soak in this ethereal vision for about two seconds.

"C'mon lazy bones," he yelped. "Didn't you hear the breakfast bell? If you don't get moving you'll miss breakfast!"

"But it feels so good under the covers, Counselor Dick," I yawned. "Can't you just stand there while I wake up? I'm a slow waker-upper."

"Sorry young lady, it's time for your debut. You're going to meet your fellow nudists!" At that, Dick yanked the covers off my naked body. That gave me goose bumps where I'd never known goose bumps before.

"Y-yes, okay, I'm g-getting up," I said between my chattering teeth. That's when I realized I was a full-fledged nudist, which didn't seem to phase Dick, but I was still adjusting to my new social, non-sexual nudist lifestyle, and too groggy to think about what it all meant.

"Do I n-need to bring anything w-with me?" I shivered, not knowing what else to say.

"Just a towel, your sandals, and sunglasses. That's it. Oh, and a word to the wise, Paloma. It's going to be 89 degrees and sunny out there today.

Most newbies don't know what can happen on their first day of full sun exposure. Remember, you're coming from a clothed world to one that's completely unclothed. You'll need to transition to avoid serious sunburn. I have sun tan oil, if you forgot to bring your own. To get you started, I can take care of your back. Believe me, you do not want to get sunburned, and your pale skin looks like it's barely seen the light of day. I do see some faint tan lines in the appropriate areas, though."

Dick was far too pragmatic about this, I mused. Was I the only nudist in Sunland with sexual, anti-social thoughts? Was it because this was my first day as a nudist? As far as Dick was concerned, I was nothing more than a pot roast in need of basting. Can I adjust to this social, non-sexual lifestyle? Hell, who cared?

"You're my camp counselor, Dick. Show me the ropes," I purred, and turned my backside for lubrication.

His hands were strong and sure of themselves. I wondered if he did this for all the newbies on their first day out. Gently but firmly he massaged down, down, down to the small of my back, where he stopped abruptly at the dimples above my butt cheeks.

I gurgled: "Keep going, Dick, if you think it will help." He didn't.

"You can reach those all by yourself, Paloma. Remember: give special attention to places where the sun doesn't shine, if you get my drift. Those are the most sensitive areas for overexposure. We'd better get a move on before we miss breakfast."

I slathered sun tan oil over my butt, legs, breasts, even where the sun doesn't shine. Dick studied my progress approvingly. As I rubbed in the oil, I imagined how my fans at Andy Wong's Sky Room would have paid dearly for this performance. But Dick wasn't interested in the glory of my perky pair of 34Ds dripping in oil. He was worried we were late for breakfast.

"Good job! This is what you'll do every morning before you leave the cabin, Paloma. Now, let's get down to the Mess Hall."

Every girl knows there's a surefire way to find out what a guy's intentions are, and it's much easier to see when he's naked. When Dick looked the other way, I peeked. Not even a quiver! Evidently, Dick was on the level; a nudist through and through, just like the book described.

Before I could think of an excuse to go back to bed, Dick grabbed my hand and dragged me into the wide world of public nudism. I was outdoors in broad daylight without a stitch of clothing on, glistening from head to toe in sun tan oil. My inner textile self told me that a cop was about to pop out from behind a tree and slap the cuffs on me. This social, non-sexual lifestyle would take some getting used to. And on top of that, I was about to be introduced to the entire clothing free community!

We entered through the Mess Hall's double doors. It looked like any large auditorium. A stage at the far end suggested it also served as a theater and lecture hall. Seated at a long, U-shaped table, scores of naked people ate their breakfast, yakking loudly at one another across the table.

The sight of so many naked people was unsettling, especially when all eyes turned in our direction. Little pinpricks danced all over my bare body.

Everyone shouted: "Good morning, Dick!"

"And good morning to you!" Dick replied. "I'd like you to meet Miss Paloma. She's from San Francisco, and it's her first nudist experience. Let's give her a big Sunland welcome."

"HI, MISS PALOMA!" they all cheered. I gave them a half-hearted wave and cracked a smile that came nowhere near their enthusiasm. All at once, they returned to their meals. Thankfully, that took the pressure off.

It was an eclectic group of ages and sexes. Children from seven to seventeen sat with their parents. Half the vacationers were couples over 50, another quarter were young families, and the other 25 percent were singles. Of the singles, females held the edge, and I just added to it.

Dick found two empty seats. He took his towel and smoothed it on the chair before he sat. I followed his lead. This was nudist etiquette 101: never sit without your towel.

A red-haired teenage girl with braids, her face, arms, and chest flecked with freckles, carried a silver tray under her bouncy breasts. She brought pancakes and scrambled eggs. No meat. For health reasons, Sunland was a meatless camp, Dick explained.

"Hi, Paloma," the red-haired girl greeted. "I'm Rochelle. If you need anything during mealtimes, just ask. I'll take care of you." She laid out our plates and coffee mugs on the table. Rochelle, I later learned, was a student at Pasadena City College. In return for free room and board at Sunland, she helped with camp chores. In the morning she served meals. Sometimes she filled in at the general store, but the rest of the day was hers to do as she pleased. She appeared to be quite popular with the teen boys at the camp.

With Dick sitting on one side of me, that left an unfamiliar face on the other side. It belonged to one Edwina Trench, a 50-something woman with silver threads amongst dark brown hair that fell midway down her back. She had heavy breasts and a round face etched in a permanent smile.

"Hello, honey," she said through a mouth full of French toast. "My name's Edwina, but everyone calls me Ed. How do you like our little family so far?"

"This is only my first day." I replied. "I'm still getting used to being around so many naked people. How long did it take you to adjust, Ed?"

"Honey, me and Chick — Chick's my better half over here — have been vacationing at Sunland every summer since they opened, so it's hard to remember ever being shy around other naked people. But from what I've seen of other newbies, it only takes a day or two before they get into the swing of things. No time at all, I'd say."

Two middle-aged men stopped behind me to introduce themselves. They had potbellies and tangled chest hair. One was bald, the other had a crew cut. They, too, wore big smiles. Naked people must smile more than the general population. The one who spoke first had a tattoo of a hula girl on his left forearm.

"Miss Paloma? I'm Frank, and this is Bob. If you ever need anything fixed in your cabin, give us a call. We're the fix-it maintenance crew. We're also in charge of the lake. Well, I exaggerate. The lake takes care of itself. We're in charge of what goes on at the lake, and the sailboat, the pier, the sunbathing areas, all that good stuff. When you're up to it, come on down and go for a swim. It's the place to be on a hot August day. We've got outdoor showers down there to help you adjust to the water temp before you jump in."

"Sounds like fun, Frank," I said. "I'm sure you'll be seeing me."

After they'd finished their meals, guests began filing out, going to one of the many healthful activities Sunland had to offer. Dick and I were two of the last to go. After he'd finished his second cup of coffee, Dick stood up.

"I think you've got enough of the basics to wing it on your own today, Paloma," he said. "Why not explore the grounds? You'll find a volleyball game in progress every day of the week. Volleyball's a great icebreaker. I'll save a seat for you here at lunchtime, okay? Don't forget, when you hear the chow bell, head down here to the Mess Hall."

I didn't tell Dick that I already had plans: I was going to meet Laura Borealis on the QT. After a quick stop at my cabin to put on my jade necklace, I headed down to Sunland Lodge to learn the real reason I was here.

CHAPTER FIVE

Strolling under the fragrant pines in my birthday suit, breathing the fresh, mountain air revitalized me. The gentle breeze caressed me in all the right places, too. When I worked in the Chinatown club scene my nudity ended with a pair of pasties and a flesh-colored thong. Now I was completely free. I guess this is why nudists are hooked on outdoor nakedness. It feels great, and no one gives you a second look. Being naked in a nudist camp is perfectly normal, no hidden agendas.

I heard typewriter keys snapping ferociously as I entered the lodge. Laura Borealis sat at her weathered, roll-top desk, typing. She stopped when she heard my sandals coming her way.

"Miss Paloma! How goes it so far? Enjoying your newfound freedom?"

"I have to admit, I am," I smiled.

Borealis looked pleased. "That's the ticket! If you think about it, you've been naked since the day you were born. You've just been hiding it under all those textiles. You're back to basics now! My golf cart is out back. We'll take it to the falls. It's easier than walking."

"We can't talk here?"

Her voice lowered a notch as she spoke.

"Maybe it's just my imagination, dear, but I have this nagging feeling that I'm being watched. Shall we go?"

Parked under a rustic lean-to behind the lodge, the golf cart took some coaxing to get started. It coughed a few times, but Miss Laura seemed unperturbed. She pulled out the choke and thumbed the starter button. When the tiny engine fired, she instantly pushed the choke

The Incredible Karswell

back in. The cart sputtered to life in a cloud of noxious fumes and we were off — at a top speed of five miles per hour. A brisk walk would have been faster, and far less noisy.

She drove past the Mess Hall, the Rec Hall, the swimming pool, and volleyball court. Dick was right. A lively volleyball match, gals vs. guys, was already in progress. It's amazing how much

more movement you see when the players are naked. Miss Laura waved and honked and everyone waved back. They, too, were smiling. It's what nudists do.

Buildings began to thin out as the road narrowed on an uphill grade. The motor labored as the road continued to climb. After a mile or so of dense pine forest on either side of us, the road dead ended in a clearing with an impressive waterfall. This was our destination. As she killed the motor, the endless roar of the waterfall filled the void.

"Welcome to Karswell Falls," she said. "We can talk here. Even if someone were nearby, they couldn't hear us through the sound of the falls."

Either Borealis had serious concerns about spies, or she was seriously paranoid. Her need for caution seemed excessive. Was Sunland Vacation Camp a den of Commie spies listening to her every word?

"Okay, Miss Laura," I said. "In my official capacity as your private investigator I'd like to know one thing — why all the secrecy?"

She answered with another question.

"Have you ever watched Karswell's Future Forecasts on television?" she asked.

"Who hasn't?" I replied. "The Incredible Karswell is everyone's favorite Hollywood psychic. Sometimes I read his newspaper column in the Chronicle."

"He doesn't like the word psychic, dear," she frowned. "He prefers 'futurist.' Semantics, he believes, is what keeps him out of trouble with the law. Anyway, I'll cut to the chase. Jerome Karswell is my husband."

Karswell Falls

"I see. So your desire for secrecy has to do with him?"

"That is correct. And when I tell you our predicament, you'll understand our need for discretion. As odd as it may sound, he has an image to uphold."

"So, Borealis is your maiden name?"

"Oh no, it was my stage name from a time when I was an aspiring actor. Jerome was too; an actor, I mean. That was 15 years ago. We met through our theater work. He wasn't a futurist then, not until he began writing down his predictions and giving them to a few local newspapers. Before we knew it, his predictions became a column. It became so popular it went into syndication.

"It's strange how it all came about. Jerome was walking along Broadway in downtown Los Angeles. A Tuesday, if I remember, in 1947. He was jaywalking across the street when a Good Humor truck hit him. He spent an entire week in the hospital, unconscious. When he finally snapped out of it, he had the gift of foretelling the future. He began schmoozing at Hollywood parties and making contacts, impressing celebrities with his predictions. He met a television producer who offered him a 15-minute slot at a local TV station two nights a week. The show took off like gangbusters. After that, we weren't stage hams anymore; he'd become a Hollywood personality."

I stopped her there. "My next question is, how'd you end up managing Sunland nudist camp? I don't see the connection."

"I was coming to that," she said. "The money began rolling in, and Jerome has always been a good businessman. He began to invest. One of his pet predictions has always been about nudism. Jerome believes nudism is the wave of the future; that one day all red-blooded Americans will spend their vacations at nudist camps for their health and wellbeing. He also predicted genital jewelry. We'll see about that one.

"In any case, Jerome decided that opening a nudist camp was the thing to do, so we purchased the Sunland property six years ago. The plan was to showcase the health benefits of nudism. As for me, my acting career ended when his career took off. I got bored sitting on the sideline, cheering him on during his rise to stardom. So, when he purchased Sunland I volunteered to run it. It gave me something to do. Besides, I've been a fan of nudism for years.

"When I'm here during the summer season, I rarely see Jerome. He stays in LA to hobnob with clients, many of whom are big name stars. They come to him for his predictions and advice, and pay dearly for them."

I said: "Okay, that brings me up to speed. Now, why do you need a private investigator?"

"Well, things changed when Jerome's family coffin disappeared."

"You mean it was stolen? Who was in it?"

"It was empty at the time, but Jerome sleeps in it occasionally. Mostly when he's agitated. It calms him, he says. It belonged to his grandfather, Cranston Karswell. You see, grandfather Karswell was a thanatophobiac — that means he had an extreme fear of death. It developed into an obsession about being buried alive. This was indeed a problem. The Karswells come from a long line of morticians. Growing up in the family funeral business, Cranston spent much of his boyhood among corpses. As far as we've been able to determine, that was what brought on his thanatophobia.

"But, he came up with a solution. He made an escape coffin. He had a wireless set installed in a side compartment within easy reach. It operated on the police bandwidth, so he could call the authorities if he woke up one day and to find he'd been buried alive. The coffin had a

It's the only place he can relax.

purple, diamond pleated lining made of satin, and was made with the finest Indonesian mahogany."

"Back up a minute," I said. "Your husband sleeps in it?"

"Yes, that's right. Sometimes I think it's a stunt. He's posed for photographs in it. He tells reporters he sleeps better when he's in the coffin, but my theory is, he wants to prove he's not afraid, like his grandfather was. Of death, I mean. Oh, and besides Sunland, Jerome owns several funeral parlors throughout the Los Angeles area. It's a Karswell family tradition."

"But if his grandfather built the coffin, why isn't he buried in it?"

"We had him cremated."

"Oh. Please go on."

Well, last month, the coffin disappeared. Jerome was having the satin lining replaced at the upholstery shop. The shop was burglarized, and Jerome's coffin was the only thing taken. All very strange."

"The coffin must have been the target, then," I said. "I don't suppose you have a photo of it?"

"Of course I do! I took it last year. Jerome was having his evening martini. He often laid in the coffin during his martini hour."

She reached behind the seat and pulled out a manila envelope with an 8x10 glossy inside. The coffin had KARSWELL lettered in mother of pearl along the side. Jerome was in it, martini in hand. He was also smoking a cigarette. He looked rested.

"We must find that coffin, Miss Paloma," Borealis pleaded. "The owner of the upholstery shop reported the theft to the police, but a casket theft is not one of their highest priorities. To them it's just a casket, not the *Karswell* casket."

"Where do you live when you're not here at Sunland, Miss Laura?"

"In downtown Los Angeles, in the Bunker Hill area. Jerome converted a hotel there and renamed it the 'Karswell Arms.' We keep an apartment there and rent out the other rooms to long-term tenants. Naturally, during the summer season I'm here at Sunland. But we close for the winter on Labor Day. We open again on Memorial Day, but Gatekeeper stays on as our caretaker. I check in with Jerome now and then during the summer months, just to keep track of him."

"When was the last time you checked in?"

"About a month ago."

This had to be the strangest client interview I'd ever had. Not only was my client naked, I was too. Just two naked women in a golf cart discussing a coffin, with a waterfall to keep eavesdroppers from listening.

I said: "I get the feeling there's more to this story."

She lowered her voice.

"You're very perceptive, Miss Paloma. You ask all the right questions. Yes, that was just the beginning. Not too long after the coffin disappeared, people I had never seen before began working at Jerome's Altadena funeral parlor — very shady looking customers if you ask me."

"That isn't strange in itself is it?" I countered. "I mean, maybe he needed the help and these two just look a bit, well, shady?"

"There's something else," she continued. "As you can see from our secluded location and the narrow road leading up to the camp's front gate, few cars other than those of our guests use it. Once in a while we get a car full of teenage boys who want to sneak a peek at what goes on here. Gatekeeper shoos them off without much fuss.

"But not long after the coffin disappeared, Gatekeeper began to notice a black Buick driving up the road. From what he's told me, there are two rough-looking characters in that car. After awhile, they drive back down the road. He's seen them several times. We have no idea what their purpose is, since they don't seem interested in the camp."

"What's up the road?"

"That's just it, nothing, as far as I know. The road dead-ends several miles beyond the gate. It's nothing more than an access road for the county fire department."

I said: "And Gatekeeper says it's the same two men, driving the same car each time?"

"That's right."

"Next time Gatekeeper sees that car, would you ask him to write down the license plate number? My partner has a contact at motor vehicles. He'll find out who owns that car."

Which reminded me — I forgot to give Alex a call when I checked in last night. It was Dick's fault. He's such a distraction. Laura had given me enough information to start work, so I suggested we return to camp. It was getting on toward lunchtime, and Dick said he was saving a seat for me at the Mess Hall. I wouldn't want to be late.

CHAPTER SIX

iss Laura dropped me off at the Mess Hall, where I found Dick waiting for me. After our meal of baked tofu, acorn squash, and brown rice, with a carrot juice chaser, Dick sent me on my way. Somehow he had the impression I'd spent all morning soaking in the hot tub, since that's what I told him. He suggested I explore the library, and put in a little "me" time poolside to work on my "no tan line" look. But before all that, I had to make a phone call.

There were two telephone booths in the lobby, and one was being used. Other than mailed letters and postcards, these two public phones were our only contact with the outside world. I slipped into the empty booth, dialed, and asked the operator to connect me with San Francisco General Hospital. "And operator, would you reverse the charges, please?"

She patched me through to the hospital switchboard, where I asked for Alexander Blade's room. After several rings, he finally picked up.

"Y'ello?"

"Alex? It's me."

"Me?"

"Your partner."

"Oh. You mean the one who closed the office so she could take a vacation? Paloma?"

"That's what I said. Me. How's the leg, tough guy?"

"Still hanging from the ceiling last time I checked. Did you know they force me to take a sponge bath every day in this pill palace? And guess who gives it to me? The cutest blonde nurse you ever wrapped your peepers around."

"Got it. A sponge bath shifts your gears — and you complain about me being on vacation, which, by the way, isn't a vacation at all. I'm working a case."

"A case?"

"Yes, you know — that thing we do to pay bills you're always complaining about? If all goes well, this one will keep us in won ton soup for a couple months."

"Tell me more, Moon Cakes. You have five whole minutes before Nurse Ilsa wheels in the sponge."

"Nurse Ilsa? Oh, never mind. You might as well hear this from me than through the grapevine. I'm in a phone booth, and I'm butt naked."

"Naked? In a phone booth? You can get arrested for that!"

"Not here, Hawkshaw. Sunland is a nudist colony. No clothing allowed."

That's when it got real quiet on the other end of the line. Finally, Alex said: "So, you gave up a naked dancing career to flaunt your feminine charms for free? Does that make sense to you?"

"Look," I growled. "I had no idea this was a nudist camp until I got here. But I don't mind telling you, Alex, it's great! It's strictly a social, non-sexual setting of like-minded people. No hanky panky allowed. And no ogling of my feminine charms either, not like the Sky Room where men couldn't take their eyes off my moving parts. I like it here."

"Oh, you do, do you?"

"I have my own camp counselor, too. He's been teaching me what the nudist lifestyle is all about."

"And you've got your own camp counselor, too. My, my."

I brought you a new sponge, Alex.

"Stop right there, Buster! I can hear that brain of yours grinding out all sorts of lurid, anti-social thoughts. Dick is strictly on the up and up. You can get tossed out of here for unseemly behavior. No COGs allowed."

"COGs?"

"Creepy Old Geezers."

"Oh, so now you speak nudist. Next thing I know you'll be passing out leaflets in Union Square about the joys of air baths."

"Moving on, Alex. The reason I'm calling is to update you on my new case. Our client is Laura Borealis; she's the camp administrator here. There've been some strange goings-on involving her husband, the Incredible Karswell, you know, the famous Hollywood psychic? His casket went missing and she wants me to find it."

"And your client's nude, too? I mean, naked?"

"Of course she is, but that has nothing to do with the case, Alex. She's a paying client. Jeez Louise! Isn't about it time for your sponge bath?"

"How right you are, Kitten! Here comes Nurse Ilsa now."

"With a sponge in one hand and you in the other," I groused. "Okay, have as much fun as the nurses' union allows, Alex. I'll keep you posted."

I hung up the phone, leaving Alex in Nurse Ilsa's capable hands. As I exited the phone booth, I noticed some fellow nudists seated on three sofas arranged in a semi-circle. They huddled around the television, a Dumont Wave Master with a twelve-inch picture tube. The blank screen told me it had not been turned on. Perky college student Rochelle sat next to a lithe, teen boy about her age. Edwina and Chick, and Bob and Frank were there, and a few married couples with small children.

I walked up to the group and asked Edwina: "What's all the hubbub?"

"It's almost eight-thirty, Hon, time for Karswell's Future Forecast! Wouldn't miss it for the world."

As the minute hand on the lobby's grandfather clock closed in on 8:29, Laura Borealis walked up to the set and turned it on while everyone held their collective breath. The tubes warmed, the screen lit up, and the deep-throated sound of a pipe organ flowed from the speaker.

An enthusiastic voice warbled: "It's that time again, folks! Time for Karswell's Future Forecast! Brought to you by Halo Shampoo. Remember, soap dulls your hair, Halo glorifies it!"

Then came the Halo Shampoo jingle: "Halo everybody, Halo! Halo Shampoo, Halo!"

"Also brought to you by," the disembodied voice continued, "Karswell's Chapel of the Chimes, with locations in East Hollywood,

Altadena, San Gabriel, and coming soon, Studio City. Remember, your future is assured when you choose Karswell's Chapel of the Chimes."

I found an empty easy chair with a clean towel and sank back into the cushion to watch the show. The titles cut to a studio set and the camera began a long, slow zoom in on Jerome Karswell seated behind a desk. A fan-like pattern of lights glowed on the wall behind him. He wore a sport coat that glittered in the light, but his tie was dark and subdued. His wavy hair, as white as marshmallow cream pie, was combed back except for a well-placed spit curl on his forehead. A spotlight angled above his head produced an angelic glow.

He had a pale, untroubled face, as if the worries of the world had never touched it. This imparted a corpse-like continence that was hard not to notice. The lobby audience hushed as Karswell began to forecast.

"Greetings my friends," he intoned in a voice like a street corner preacher, "We are all interested in the future, for that is where you and I will spend the rest of our lives. And remember, my friends, future events such as these will affect you in the future!

"My friends, it may shock you to learn that a great American city will succumb to a terrible virus from outer space. This virus will turn solids into a jelly-like substance. Buildings — without warning — will collapse, trapping thousands in the rubble. Trains, cars, and busses will be useless. Factories will be unable to continue production. Doctors in the midst of surgery will find their instruments useless. Hypodermics will not penetrate skin, but will bend on contact. I forecast that the name of this city is Minneapolis, Minnesota. The year? October 29, 1988."

I crossed my legs and calculated it would take another 37 years before Karswell's space virus wiped out Minneapolis. It was a safe enough prediction. He droned on from there.

"In the year 1999 your home will no longer have chairs, it will only have reclining couches! Science will have convinced you that sitting is bad for you, and that a reclining position is best! One other valuable lesson in the coming 48 years is that liquid food is healthier than solid, fried food! Your pantry will consist of three or four jars of tiny pellets, which you can boil in water giving you soups, stews or meats. If you are wise, you will be living on a liquid diet!

"I forecast a revolutionary new embalming fluid will preserve your body for the ages. Your remains will be dressed in a state-of-the-art fiberglass garment and placed in a fiberglass casket. It will endure the elements as long as time itself. Your body will become a temple that is preserved forever, even after life on earth has ceased. In the distant future, people from another planet may one day gaze upon your life-like remains. We are about to patent this incredible process for the Karswell Chapel of the Chimes. Ask one of our chapel directors when it will become available for your loved ones.

"I forecast that in the year 1999 you will awake to a darkened world where the sun will not shine because atomic radiation from nuclear bomb tests will have risen into the outer orbit of the earth and become solidified. It will form an opaque umbrella that keeps sunlight from reaching us!

"Our major engineering feat of 1999 will be guided missiles to disperse this horrifying nightmare. I forecast we will again have sunlight, and the engineers of 1999 will be successful! Forty-eight years will pass quickly, so stand by!"

Thankfully, a Halo Shampoo commercial interrupted Karswell's nightmarish predictions. When he returned, he wrapped up the show on a lighter note.

"I forecast that it will only be a matter of time before you join a nudist camp or health farm to enjoy the complete freedom of nudity! The human body is nothing to be ashamed of, my friends, as we were all born in the likeness of God. It will be in your lifetime that you will walk down the street, you will shop, and attend the theater in the nude, perhaps even sooner than you think."

"Hear, hear!" the room cheered.

"I forecast that education will be given to children through television, not personal teachers, but there will be a warden on duty to make sure that student interest is maintained. Later, memory pills will give students all the education they can possibly use!"

The more outrageous Karswell's forecasts became, the louder the organ music got, until it came time to end.

"Remember, my friends, we are all but weary travelers on the highway of life, plodding on to our endless existence. Find the nearest Chapel of the Chimes Funeral Parlor today, for a worry free, eternal tomorrow."

I decided Karswell's Future Forecast was almost as good as a sleeping pill. I was ready for bed by the time Miss Laura turned off the set, and it was only 8:45. My fellow nudists began filing out, returning to their cabins. Borealis beckoned me to come into her office.

She said: "You heard Jerome's forecast about the fiberglass caskets and such? That's only one invention his research and development team has been working on."

I replied: "Karswell's Future Forecasts seems like a great way to plug his funeral homes."

"Yes, but even I don't know the half of what he's up to," she said, frowning. "I do know he has a research lab where the experiments take place, but beyond that, I hear of these new inventions like everyone else. If you sift through the pabulum he dishes out, sometimes you'll hear an actual story."

At that, her face went limp as she began her impression of the Incredible Karswell.

"My friends," she moaned in a low voice, "I forecast that one day we will fill your everlasting temple with helium. You will become a fireproof zeppelin, which will endure the rigors of outer space. Your earthly coil will float forever among the stars, long after the earth is no more."

"That's hilarious!" I said. "You should have your own TV show. Is that a real thing, this new embalming fluid he talked about?"

"Yes, it is," she replied. "I saw a brochure Jerome had printed up about it. I expect they'll be handed out to customers at his funeral homes. He wants to become the Knott's Berry Farm of funeral parlors. I bet you didn't know his East Hollywood location looks like a Victorian undertaker's parlor, or that his Altadena location looks like a Medieval Bavarian house. The San Gabriel parlor is done up like a giant Chinese pagoda."

"He certainly is a showman," I said. "And all this stuff comes from his secret research lab?"

"That's right," Borealis said. "Lord knows where it is."

"It might be closer than you think, Miss Laura. Where would you put a secret lab? Not in downtown Los Angeles. You'd look for a remote location, far from prying eyes. How about a members' only nudist camp? What better place than right here in Sunland!"

CHAPTER SEVEN

 was up and out of bed, but not dressed — why would I be? — when I heard the screen door slam on Dick's cabin next door. A tall shadow with a determined stride passed by my front window.

I stepped out onto my front porch and yelled: "Where you headed, Dick?" He stopped.

"Oh, hi, Paloma. I'm going to the lake. Bob asked me to double check the new electric motor he installed on the sailboat."

"Mind if I tag along?"

"Sure thing! It'll be great having company."

I wanted to find Karswell's secret laboratory, which, I deduced, must be somewhere on the Sunland property. Down by the lake would be a good place to start, and who better to help me find it than Dick.

"Can you hang on a sec?" I said. "I need to slip on my sandals. Do you think I'll need sun tan oil today?" I waited for the response I knew was coming.

"Always, Paloma! That should be your morning ritual before you ever leave the cabin. Did you read the poster I put on your bathroom door? The Do's and Don'ts of Sunbathing?"

"What poster?" Of course I saw it, but I wanted to see how far I could take this.

Dick forgot all about the lake and vaulted onto my front porch. I opened the screen door and he marched into the sitting room. It looked like I was about to get one of his nudist lectures.

"Into the bathroom, kiddo!" he ordered. "I'm sure I put a poster on your bathroom door. You should have seen it."

He herded me through the bedroom into the tiny bathroom where we squeezed in. He shut the door behind us.

"Yep, there it is," he said, pointing to the thumb tacked poster on the door. "It's behind the bath towel you hung in front of it. Since we're here, I might as well go over the important points with you. German scientists came up with this list in the '20s. It's a little known fact that the Germans started what we now call the nudist movement."

With barely an inch between us, Dick's body heat felt like an electric blanket on my bare skin. I forgot all about the secret laboratory, Karswell, even the missing coffin. All I wanted was to pad this moment for all I could get.

Vacuously, I replied: "The Germans? I didn't realize the Nazis spent their free time in nudist colonies."

Dick frowned. "That's because Hitler banned them when he came to power. Nudism was not his thing. He had only one testicle, you know. Maybe that had something to do with it."

"Gee, only one testicle," I mused. "No wonder he was angry all the time."

I began sweating like the proverbial snowball in hell, which was probably where I was going for pulling a stunt like this on Dick.

I edged even closer to his six foot three inch frame, standing on my tiptoes to peer over his shoulder. That pushed my sweaty pair of 34Ds up against his back. He didn't seem to notice, and began reading the poster.

"*One*: never sunbathe unless the temperature is above 64 degrees. You won't have a problem with that here, Paloma. *Two*: wait at least two hours after a meal before sunbathing. *Three*: on your first nude day in the sun, stay out no more than five minutes, then increase the time five minutes each day thereafter."

He stopped and thought for a moment. "Don't worry about that one, Paloma. We can increase that time by applying plenty of premium sun tan oil. *Four*: rest in the shade for at least 15 minutes after your sunbath. And, last but not least, take a shower after your sunbath, then rest for at least half an hour."

"Sounds like good advice," I purred. "From now on it's plenty of sun tan oil for me. Speaking of that, I might need some help, you know, with my back?"

"No problem," Dick said agreeably.

If it got any hotter in here, I'd pass out. He scooted me back, opened the door and let the fresh mountain air rush in. We fled to the sitting room where I could breathe again.

I'd purchased a bottle of Coppertone at the camp's general store. Rochelle, the freckle faced student I'd met earlier, worked part time there. She recommended Coppertone, used it herself, she said. She didn't look burned to me, maybe just a little pink, so I purchased a bottle.

"Here you go," I said, handing Dick the bottle. "I have my own lotion this time. Now, if you wouldn't mind?"

I turned around to give him full access to my backside. My anticipation began to wane as I stood there far too long, waiting for the feel of firm hands on my shoulders. I turned to find him reading the label on the back of the bottle.

At last, he quipped: "You know, Paloma, my tanning oil is imported from Italy. It's got more UV protection than yours. Let me run next door and get it, okay?"

"You're swell, Dick," I cooed as sweet as maple syrup.

I sensed these oil sessions had become my version of Alex's sponge bath obsession, but what the hell. I'm on vacation and I'll have as much fun as Dick is willing to dish out. He returned in less than two shakes of a white tailed rabbit with the sun tan oil.

"Ok, Paloma, ready?"

Again, I bared my backside. Dick began the methodical lube job I was becoming so fond of. His hands — strong and confident — worked their way down to the dimples above my butt cheeks, then stopped. Damn!

"Ok, the rest is up to you, kid," he said, handing me the bottle.

I took over, begrudgingly. After two days of practice, I was already pretty good at this. In fact, I finished in no time. I grabbed my cartwheel hat, sunglasses, sandals, and Chinese jade necklace.

"I'm ready," I announced, and we were off on our clothing free hike.

Bob and Frank had said the lake was a popular place most days, but it was still early, with a slight chill in the air. We were the only guests in sight.

The lake wasn't enormous. The opposite side didn't look that far off. Cattails lined the shoreline, with thickets and trees beyond those. A narrow wooden pier no more than four feet wide jutted out over the water, with a small sailboat tied at the end.

"We'll give the boat the once over," Dick said. "Frank installed a battery-powered motor for the days when there's no wind. He said it's only a five horsepower job. Nothing crazy; just enough power for a lake this size."

I followed Dick to the end of the pier, where we stopped to look down at the boat.

"Want to take her out for a spin?" he asked. "I want to be sure everything works as it should before guests start using it."

Dick stepped down into the boat. He held up his hand for mine. I grabbed onto it and hopped in.

The motor had a simple mechanism: an ignition key and a speed lever. I sat in the rear and held the rudder. Dick hooked up the battery, turned on the ignition and we started out. From the pier we went buzzing around the lake, sailing in circles, back and forth, sometimes following the shoreline, until we reached the far end of the lake.

Dick listened intently to the hum of the motor the entire time, while I steered.

"This is the life," I said at last, stretching out my legs. "It's going to be hard to go back to the outside world again."

Dick laughed. "I know what you mean," he said. "It's something we all go through at the end of every summer vacation. It's like being on parole, and then all of a sudden you're thrown back in jail with your prison clothes on again. Feels like losing your freedom. It'll take a couple of weeks to readjust."

Being alone with Dick on the lake seemed like a good time to learn more about him. When he's not being a nudist, he must be something else. However, Miss Laura said personal inquiries are not allowed. "Ask no questions about your fellow guests," she said. "We go by first names only," she said. But here, on the lake, it felt like rules were meant to be broken.

"I hope I'm not prying, Dick," I began cautiously, "but what are you when you're not being a camp counselor here at Sunland?"

Dick looked away from the clouds overhead, shot a serious look my way, then smiled.

"We're not supposed to discuss our personal lives on the outside, but if you don't tell Miss Laura, I won't. I'm an architect by trade. In fact, I graduated from Stanford last year. I was quarterback on the football team, and was a member of the university boxing club.

"After Pearl Harbor, I enlisted in the Marines when I was 17. They shipped me out from San Diego to the Pacific Theater. Got wounded in Iwo Jima in March of 1945, so Uncle Sam shipped me home again. Soon as I could, I enrolled at Stanford, graduated, and joined my dad's firm in Pasadena. My parents are dedicated nudists as far back as I can remember. They're into health foods, too. You might say we aren't your average American family.

"I've vacationed at Sunland every summer since they opened, but I'm afraid nudism is a difficult subject for outsiders to grasp. They think we're hedonists, even Socialists, rebelling against the capitalist system. That's why I don't discuss it with non nudists. I doubt most of our guests do, either, and I would advise you to do the same. Would you like to hear my theory on what you do in the outside world?"

"I'm all ears," I smiled.

"I think you're a model."

"A model? What gave you that idea?"

"You have the figure and the looks for it, and, well, I couldn't help but notice, and I hope you're not offended, Paloma, but it's your pubic hair. You don't have any! I thought maybe you modeled swimwear or underclothing, and have to keep it that way. As you've probably noticed, women here at Sunland let theirs go natural. You stand out in more ways than one."

I had to think fast. I couldn't tell him I started the Brazilian waxing habit as a nude dancer in a Chinatown strip club. That would tarnish my social, non-sexual nudist image. And I sure couldn't tell him I was an undercover PI working a case here in Sunland. So, I fibbed.

"It's an old Chinese custom," I said. "Actually, I'm a secretary at a San Francisco detective agency." That was my second fib, but less egregious than the first. "It's interesting work," I babbled, "hearing about cases and talking to clients. I enjoy it. I grew up in a small town on the Sacramento delta."

So much for trust and openness; except for the part about the delta, I was lying like a throw rug.

Dick listened intently to the hum of the motor.

"That does sound interesting," Dick replied. "Most of the jobs I get are for custom designed bungalows, but once in a while something fun comes along, like, anything over four stories. I keep hearing how Bunker Hill will be torn down one day and completely redesigned. I'm hoping we'll be part of the rebuilding, when the city finally approves it."

Our chitchat meandered on like this as we sailed back to the pier. The other guests must have gone swimming in the pool today, because the beach was still empty.

I steered the boat closer to the pier as Dick turned the speed control to STOP. We drifted the rest of the way. He held my hand to steady me as I stepped up to the pier. From the pier I leaned back down to return the favor by pulling him up. With one foot on the pier and one still in the boat, Dick's leg must have brushed against the speed control lever. That engaged the motor and the boat lurched away from the pier. He'd forgot to turn off the ignition!

Dick fell straight back, striking his head against the boat. Worse, his leg tangled in the boat's tie up rope. With no one at the helm, the boat began dragging him unconscious through the water toward the middle of the lake.

I dove in. Dick's lungs would be full of water and I didn't know how much time he had left. I was closing the gap between us when the boat began a slow U turn back in my direction; a big break. I closed the distance faster. Pulling myself up alongside the runaway boat I grabbed the lever to stop the motor, then dove under to find Dick. He wasn't far below. I untangled his foot and pulled him to the surface. Five minutes later, I had him ashore, but he wasn't breathing.

I flipped him onto his back and pulled his arms above his head, then compressed them against his chest, back and forth, the Silvester resuscitation method. I learned it in life saving class, and it wasn't working. So, I tried something I'd only read about. I pulled his jaw down with my thumb, checked the position of his tongue to make sure he hadn't swallowed it, and began blowing air into his mouth. After each breath, I compressed his chest hard several times with both hands clasped. I kept this up, hoping someone would see us and send for help.

If this had happened in the textile world, we would have been wearing our swimsuits. But Dick and I were naked. It was impossible not to have physical contact. My chest pressed against his as I breathed into his mouth. The Sunland rulebook strictly forbids physical contact in public, but this was a social, non-sexual emergency. That kooky thought left my mind as Dick's body convulsed and he coughed up water. His eyes opened. They looked even bluer than I remembered.

"Just lie still, Dick," I said.

"Paloma?" he said, coughing. "What happened? I remember falling into the water. How'd I get here?"

"I brought you in," I said. "You hit your head on the boat and it dragged into the lake. But you're okay now."

"Y-you — saved my l-life!"

"Hey, I was a lifeguard at the Isleton public swimming pool after school. That's where I learned lifesaving techniques."

Now that I knew he was safe I remembered how good he felt as I held onto him in the water. Then, a voice broke in. Frank and Bob had returned.

Frank eyed us suspiciously.

"Say, what goes on here, you two?" Then he realized something was wrong. "Dick? Are you all right?"

I explained what had just happened. Frank sent Bob back to camp for Miss Laura's golf cart. "Just take it easy, Dick," Frank ordered. "We'll have the nurse check you out at the lodge, then Bob will take you back to your cabin."

Frank then turned to me. "That was a brave thing you did, Miss Paloma. You saved our favorite camp counselor!"

"Mine, too," I replied.

By the time Bob arrived with the golf cart Dick was already sitting up, nursing the goose egg on his head. They helped him into the cart and Bob drove back at top speed, which was still five miles an hour. Frank and I watched as the cart disappeared up the dirt road.

"I'll check on him after dinner, Frank," I said. "It's a very nice lake."

My sandals were on the pier, right where I'd left them. I slipped them on and began walking back to my cabin. I didn't bother to towel off.

CHAPTER EIGHT

hat evening I went next door to Owl Cottage to check on Dick before Lights Out. I knocked. His door was always unlocked so I went right in. He was lying in bed, reading.

"Feeling better?" I chirped, standing next to his bed.

He smiled. "Yes, much better, thanks. I was just thinking about you, Paloma. You sure are full of surprises."

"I am?"

"Yes," he replied. "Besides working as a secretary at a detective agency, you're a strong swimmer and know all about rescue and resuscitation methods. Makes me wonder what other talents you've got."

"C'mon, Dick. It's not all that surprising," I whitewashed. "It's like I told you; I grew up on the delta."

"Well, in any case I owe you one. A big one."

"Are you serious?"

"Any time, any where, you name it."

"Great! I'll collect right now. You've been vacationing in Sunland since it opened, right?"

"Yes, every August is my vacation time."

"Do you know of any remote areas around here where the average Sunland guest doesn't go?"

Dick laid his book on his chest, mulling over my question.

"Yes, there is. There's an undeveloped area where members aren't encouraged to go, mainly because it's difficult to reach. It's above Karswell Falls. It would be a real challenge for most guests to climb the cliff face, especially in the nude. And you can't bypass the cliff without leaving the property. You'd have to take the fire road up the mountain a few miles."

"Do you think Miss Laura would let you borrow the golf cart for a trip to the falls? I'd love to see it." I didn't tell him I'd already been there.

"I don't see why not. When do you want to go?"

"Whenever you're feeling up to it."

"How about tomorrow morning? We can leave right after breakfast."

The sharp chime of the lights out bell pierced the darkness outside the cabin. After saying our goodnights, I left Dick to his book and returned to Jaybird Cottage. Within fifteen minutes, I had fallen into a deep, dreamless sleep.

• • •

I ignored the breakfast bell and slept in. True to his word, Dick came to my cabin after he had finished his breakfast. When I opened my eyes Dick was towering over me like a California redwood. I don't mind telling you, it was a pleasant sight.

"Am I late for breakfast?" I yawned.

"You missed it."

I threw off the covers, stretched my arms high above my head, turned and put my feet on the floor.

"Make yourself at home," I said. "I'll brush my teeth and pick out my clothes. Ha ha."

That was a nudist joke. Mornings at Sunland meant I didn't have to squeeze into a girdle and bra, choose a dress, or put on makeup; just brush my teeth and hair. That's the beauty of nudism. If I want to go for a swim, I just dive in, no suit required. And when I climb back out, there's no sopping wet swimsuit to make me feel uncomfortable. I'm ready to greet the day as soon as I get out of bed.

When I came out of the bathroom twenty minutes later, I found Dick settled in the easy chair, reading a magazine I'd bought at the Sunland general store.

I put my hands on my hips and said, "I suppose you've applied your sun tan oil today?"

"You bet. Every morning. Never forget."

I had brought my bottle of Coppertone from the bathroom and held it out to Dick.

"How about a little help with my back?"

"Hey, it's the least I can do after yesterday! I even brought the good stuff."

Dick must have brought a case of that joy oil. I turned to give him my rear view. His fingers made magic along my shoulders, working their way down to the small of my back. Then I realized something different was happening. He continued below my waist.

First, he massaged the left cheek, then the right. He kneeled down and kept going. After imparting a rosy glow to my caboose, he caressed each thigh and calf, thoroughly massaging as he went.

"You're really getting the hang of this, Dick," I moaned. "Those UV rays won't have a chance."

When he finished my feet, I turned to offer him full frontal access to the rest of me. That's when he got cold feet again.

"Maybe you should take over from here, Paloma."

"Okay, but it was great while it lasted," I whined. "Those hands of yours are pure magic, Dick. If you did this for a living I'd be your best customer."

Dick smiled. "Did I forget to mention I worked my way through college as a sports masseur?" he said. "I guess my hands are programmed for it."

"I'll say!" I knew I was sounding far too enthusiastic. Better reel myself back in; think more about the case.

"Why, Dick! You're so full of surprises!" I joked.

Sheepishly, he gave me the bottle of oil. I rubbed it on my face, my mounded marvels, my belly, and where the sun doesn't shine. I was fully protected. Dick already had the golf cart parked outside his cabin. Donning my hat, sandals, and sunglasses, I was ready for Karswell Falls.

It was a familiar trip for me, though I didn't mention that to Dick. When we reached the falls, he parked next to a large boulder. We hopped out and walked to the shimmering pool at the base of the waterfall. I craned my neck, looking up the cliff face, shading my eyes from the morning sun.

"You've never been up there?" I asked.

"Nope, no reason to. As far as I know, there are no hiking trails, and it might be full of poison oak, the bane of any hiker, especially a naked one. Maybe you noticed the map on the wall at the lodge, the one that shows how the Sunland property ends here at the falls? Well, that's not accurate. I know for a fact the property goes back at least another half mile or more."

We sat on a flat boulder and dipped our feet into the chilly water. It was turning into a warm southern California day, but the cold water gave me the shivers. From the look on Dick's face, I could tell he had something on his mind, and I didn't want to ask what it was.

"I was wondering, Paloma," he began. "You don't seem too interested in our camp activities. I mean, you don't play volleyball or tennis, and you haven't spent much time sunbathing by the pool. Instead, you'd rather come all the way out here to Karswell Falls."

"I love waterfalls," I fibbed, feeling remorse for lying to him again. "I don't suppose there's been any odd activity around here? I mean, do you get many snoops, teenagers looking for a thrill, stuff like that?"

"You ask the oddest questions," he said. "Sure, once in a great while Gatekeeper catches kids trying to sneak in. But they're easy to catch. They park their cars near the front gate."

"But wouldn't it be more difficult to catch someone if they came in above the falls?"

"I suppose; well, sure it would," Dick said. "But they couldn't see the camp, even from that far up. It's a long way down the road, and the trees block their view. Why all this interest in the falls and snoops, Paloma?"

I was only half listening. My eyes had locked onto something in the water, caught between two rocks. I waded in up to my waist as Dick watched in confused silence. The water was ice cold, even in the heat of summer. The chill turned my nipples into bullets. I reached down and picked up — a hat! I turned and waded back to shore, massaging my legs to warm them up.

"What do you make of this, Dick?" I said, showing him what I had found.

"It looks like a Tyrolean hat. Where the heck did that come from?"

"That's a good question," I replied. "Who wears a hat like this at camp? Nobody, right? My guess is it came from up there." I pointed up the cliff.

"Well, what if it did?"

"That means Sunland has unwelcome guests, Dick!" I added a note of alarm in my voice for dramatic effect. "Could be an outsider is lurking up there, someone who belongs to this hat. A stranger, get it?"

"I see your point. If it does belong to one of the guests, Miss Laura should know. Could be there's a perfectly reasonable explanation."

"Let's find out, then," I replied, and began walking back to the golf cart.

As we bounced along the dirt road back to camp, I couldn't help but notice Dick's thigh pressed tightly against mine. Sure, we were naked, sitting even closer than we were in my Rambler on the day I arrived. But all it took was a few days of my social, non-sexual nudist life and I was feeling relaxed and anxiety free. Sure, I got the shivers every time Dick rubbed sun tan oil on me, but now we were just a couple of friendly Sunlanders, out for a healthy dose of fresh air. No more angst and mixed signals like I used to get in the textile world.

However, I did sense that Dick's near-death experience at the lake had changed his impression of me. This morning's oil treatment was far more intimate than his usual application. No matter. I had an ally, and I had the feeling I'd need one.

CHAPTER NINE

aura Borealis studied the hat as she stood behind the front desk of Sunland Lodge. She ran her fingers over its broken feather and checked the label inside.

"Alpine, Ltd.," she muttered. "That's odd. Jerome buys his Tyrolean hats from Alpine Ltd."

"Why would your husband need Tyrolean hats?" I asked.

"It's a long story," Borealis began. "Jerome came up with an idea for a new, high-end funeral package for his Altadena parlor — you know, the one that looks like an old fashioned Bavarian house? He calls it the Oktoberfest Farewell, and he charges a cool one thousand dollars per service."

"That's a hefty price tag for a trip to the hereafter," I said.

"Well, Jerome spent several months designing the Oktoberfest Farewell. It's quite a production, too, from a funeral director's standpoint. It starts with a Royal First Viewing. The loved one is dressed in a Karswell-designed slumber robe. Then there's a Second Viewing, with the guest of honor dressed in his or her everyday attire. But on the last day — the day of the funeral service — the loved one, if it's a man, is wearing lederhosen and a Tyrolean hat. If it's a woman, she's dressed in a midi length embroidered Dirndl, with a lace apron and crop top."

"Did you say, *lederhosen*? Last week, two men wearing lederhosen attacked me in a diner parking lot. Their outfits made no sense to me at the time, but I wonder if this Oktoberfest service, or those involved with it somehow, might have been connected to the attack? And now this hat magically appears at the falls. This is more than a coincidence."

"Hold it right there!" Dick yelped. "You didn't tell me you'd been attacked."

"Until now there was no reason to," I replied. "I wasn't hurt, and the two men ran off. Miss Laura, does anyone other than the corpse wear Bavarian clothing?"

"Why, yes. The ushers and other employees wear traditional Bavarian clothing during the Oktoberfest Farewell service."

"I see. The plot thickens," I said. "Would you dry this hat for me and put it somewhere safe? I'd like to go to my cabin to clean up. Shall we, Dick?"

Back in the sitting room of Jaybird Cottage the silence around Dick's presence was deafening. While I pondered the latest developments in the case, Dick's thoughts were wrestling with an entirely different subject — me.

After rocking back and forth in the rocking chair mulling things over, he finally spoke. "You know, Paloma, you've become a real mystery to me."

"What do you mean?"

"Yesterday I thought you were a secretary for a San Francisco detective agency."

"And today?"

"Today there's a lot more going on than meets the eye."

"But Dick, I'm baring everything I've got here. There's not much left to hide."

Frowning, he replied: "Okay, if that's how you want it I won't be nosy."

"Look, Dick, if I told you I was a spy, would you believe me?"

"I might."

"Well, all I can tell you right now is that I really do like you, and I'm truly grateful you've got my back. I love that part our relationship in more ways than one. But for now can we not dig in too deep, at least, not yet? I have my reasons."

"Okay. If that's how you want it, that's how it'll have to be," Dick said.

I knew he wasn't happy with my answer, but it took the pressure off.

"Thanks for being so understanding, Dick. Hey, the lunch bell rang half an hour ago. We'd better get a move on!"

I hooked my arm in his and pulled him out the door, heading for the Mess Hall. Dick was a curious guy, and smart. Hell, he was a Stanford grad. I got my diploma from the principal of Isleton High. It was only a matter of time before Dick would figure me out, maybe even blow my cover. I had to think this through, even tell him the truth at the right time. Lord knows I was tired of the white lies I'd been telling him.

We laid our mandatory towels on our seats and sat down for lunch. The menu was Brussels sprouts, nut loaf, and something akin to tofu jerky. The menu chalkboard near the front door listed vegan chocolate pie as dessert. The hall was filled with the usual crowd of non-conformist health seekers. Except for one.

Instead of perky, freckle-faced Rochelle, a tall, raven-haired woman served meals in her place. She had thick, dark hair tied behind her back in a cascading ponytail, a pleasant expression, dark eyes, sun kissed skin with no tan lines, and a mature, shapely figure. She delivered meals with panache and introduced herself as Beverly.

"Hi, Beverly, I'm Paloma. Where's Rochelle today?" I asked.

"I'm not sure," our dark haired server replied. "She didn't show up for work. I was called at the last minute to fill in."

"Has anyone seen her?"

"Not that I know of. Miss Laura would know."

I turned to Dick. "That's odd. What do you think?"

"It's not like Rochelle," he said. "She's a responsible kid. She wouldn't leave the kitchen staff in the lurch like that."

After lunch, Dick and I went in search of Miss Laura, who was never too difficult to find. She was in her office, eating lunch. She had her meals brought to the office so she could keep working. We explained our concerns about Rochelle, but she already knew about her mysterious disappearance.

"I summoned Gatekeeper," Laura said. "If Rochelle left the grounds, she had to use the front gate, and Gatekeeper is vigilant when it comes to gate security."

On questioning Gatekeeper, we learned that, to his knowledge, Rochelle had not passed through the gate. Besides, it was a long walk to the nearest city. She'd need a ride, and not a single car had left the camp.

"Dear, dear, dear," Laura Borealis fretted. "I do hate the thought of calling the sheriff about this. He'll start prying into our affairs, looking for any excuse to shut us down. The county already has it in for us, thanks to a group of preachers who accuse us of throwing wild orgies. Even worse, there are the McCarthy right-wingers. They accuse us of being Communists and Socialists. But, what choice do I have? I'll have to call the sheriff."

"Before you bring in the law, Miss Laura, let us do a little snooping first," I offered. "She's only been missing since this morning. Law enforcement would prefer to take a missing person report after 24 hours."

"Thank you, dear. I would appreciate anything you and Dick would be willing to do for us."

I said: "Didn't I see her with Jared the other day? Wasn't he the same boy she sat next to during Karswell's TV show last night?"

"That would be Jared, yes." Borealis confirmed. "Right about now you'll find him in the library, listening to music, or playing volleyball on the court."

She was right. We found Jared listening to a Les Paul and Mary Ford platter on a pair of headphones at the library. He looked about 19, tight, slender build, handsome good looks, crew cut, wearing canvas slip-on shoes. Except for the one place you'd expect to find it, his smooth body was hairless. He was reading the July issue of *Popular Mechanics* magazine, and was so wrapped up in what he was reading he didn't notice us enter the room.

"Hi, Jared,' Dick said. No reply. Dick tapped him on the shoulder and the kid jumped a mile.

"Holy crap!" Jared yeeped. "You scared the bejeezus out of me, Dick!" He yanked off the headphones in a huff, but his demeanor suddenly changed to calm and cool when he eyed me standing behind Dick.

In a low, suave voice, he asked: "Uhm, who's your friend, Dick?"

"Jared, this is Paloma. She's new here. Say, listen, we're trying to find Rochelle. When was the last time you saw her?"

"Rochelle? Is anything wrong?"

I broke in: "She didn't show up for her shift at the Mess Hall today, and no one seems to know where she is."

"Wow, that's not like Rochelle. The last time I saw her was this morning, early. Said she wanted to see Karswell Falls, and that I should go with her. I told her I'd tag along, but not right away 'cause I had stuff to do, dig? You know how she is when she makes up her mind. She wanted to split right away, so she'd get back in time for her shift. So, she went without me. Crazy!"

We left Jared to his music and walked back to Sunland Lodge. When we told Miss Laura what we had learned, she offered the golf cart for a trip to the falls, adding it was low on gas and how we'd better fill it up. She showed us a fifty-five gallon storage drum out back, where we siphoned out enough fuel for a round trip to the falls.

The route was becoming very familiar, this being the third time I'd ridden it in nearly as many days. An unspoken fear dogged us, fear that we'd find Rochelle injured, or worse when we got there. That thought left us when we found nothing unusual at the falls. But it made her disappearance even more mysterious.

"Let's take a look around the pool," Dick suggested.

Wading in, we reached a sandy area on the opposite side where two people might sunbathe if they sidled up close. That's where Dick found the sandal, one of Rochelle's, near the base of the falls.

"This is very strange," Dick said. "How far would she get wearing one sandal? Why didn't she put it back on?"

"Do you think she climbed the cliff face?" I asked.

"That wouldn't be easy! You can't see it from here, but there's a narrow path in the rock. Even with hiking shoes it would be a tough climb, and with one sandal missing I can't see how Rochelle could do it."

I wish we had hiking gear," I said. "A nudist could get pretty scratched up on those rocks."

"I don't think we have much choice," Dick said. "Well? I'm up for it if you are."

Dick's muscular body had no problem climbing the steep trail, but there were loose stones along the way that made it a perilous trek. We held hands, with Dick pulling me up as we continued to climb. As we reached the final stretch, I realized why this path was not for the feint of heart. The last eight feet went straight up. Dick grabbed hold of an exposed tree root to pull himself up. Safely on top, he laid on his stomach at the edge extending his hand down to me. In one quick movement he pulled me up. Our legs and arms were bleeding from cuts we endured along the way. With the possible exception of Rochelle, I thought we might well be the first naked hikers to conquer Karswell Falls.

Resting on a smooth stone above the falls, we watched the water shimmer along the creek bed until it spilled down Karswell Falls. I noticed a wooded area some twenty feet behind us, but still no sign of Rochelle. We began hiking into the woods, adding even more scratches to our legs as we traipsed through coyote brush. I just hoped we weren't walking through poison oak.

"Watch your skin for ticks," Dick warned.

"What's a tick look like?"

"It's a tiny black speck you don't want to find on your skin," he said. "It's a bug that digs into your flesh, and they're tough to get out."

"Great thought! Let's keep moving."

Edging our way through the woods for 10 minutes or so, we came to a clearing. That was our first surprise. The second was a large building in the middle of the clearing, a brick warehouse of some kind. We approached from the rear without seeing anyone, exploring its perimeter, careful not to make a sound. The front of the building ran parallel to a wall and a large wooden gate. The painted sign above the warehouse door read: "Precision Tool Company."

"Do you know anything about this place, Dick?" I whispered.

"Not a thing. I'm willing to bet Miss Laura doesn't know about it either."

"What would a tool company be doing on Sunland property?" I wondered aloud. "Unless this is Karswell's secret laboratory! Isn't that

The Precision Tool Company

the county fire road on the other side of the wall? The same road that passes by the Sunland gate?"

Our conversation ended abruptly when a woman's scream pierced the silence. It came from inside the building.

"Help!"

"That's Rochelle!" blurted Dick.

Taking a cautious look through a side window, we saw two men hunched over Rochelle's nude body holding lit cigarettes in their hands. They had her tied to a chair, and looked as though they were using the cigarettes to burn her arms.

"That does it! I'm going in," Dick roared. "Let's try the front door."

Sprinting now, we reached the door. The creeps inside must have felt safe enough to leave it unlocked. We entered into a sparsely furnished office with a desk, a phone, and a wall clock. Padding silently, we approached a door behind the desk. Dick cracked it open a few inches, just enough to hear what was going on.

"Okay, let's try this again," a deep voice grated. "You work for that private snoop from Frisco. Don't deny it! How much do you know? Come clean or we'll burn your pretty pink knockers. GIVE!"

Dick opened the door further, just wide enough for us to slip through. The two scumbags were enjoying their work so much they didn't hear us coming. But when they noticed a look of surprise on Rochelle's face, they spun around. It was over in a heartbeat.

Dick clocked the tall palooka with a solid right to the jaw. He fell back and hit the floor, out cold. I took the ugly one in the oversized cap, jabbing him in the chest with a left, then coming down hard with a right on the back of his neck. He went out like a candle in a monsoon.

Dick looked at me, incredulous. "See? That's what I mean! Where'd you learn to fight like that?"

Rochelle came to my rescue before I came up another one of my fibs.

"I can't believe you're here!" she gasped. "I thought no one would find me."

I untied her arms and legs from the chair. The burns on her forearms and shoulders told me the creeps had been working on her for some time.

"We found your sandal at the bottom of the falls," I said. "We knew you had to be nearby. What happened, Rochelle?"

Between sobs and tears, Rochelle explained: "All I wanted was to see the view from the top of the falls. I saw the path going up the side of the cliff and climbed it. My sandal fell off when I got to the very end of the path. Then those awful men grabbed me and pulled me up. They said I was a spy. They tied me to this chair and said I came from San Francisco. I told them I didn't know what they were talking about, and I really didn't. That's when they burned me. Then you came and I've never been so grateful."

"You've never seen these two before?" Dick asked her.

"Never."

"I have," I frowned.

Dick looked surprised. "You have? Where?"

"They're not wearing lederhosen this time, but these are the same two chumps that came after me at the diner last week."

Dick rolled the tall one onto his stomach.

"Let's tie them up and take a look around," he said. "It won't take long to find out if this place belongs to Karswell. Wait a minute! I saw a phone in the front office. I'll call Miss Laura and let her know we found Rochelle."

Dick sprinted to the office, where he called the lodge. He asked Miss Laura to send someone with a car to pick us up.

"Tell them to continue up the fire road till they see the Precision Tool Company building on the left," he said. "We'll be waiting by the gate."

Dick rang off, and we began to explore. We found a storage room filled with Karswell caskets in various states of construction. Some were painted in black lacquer, Chinese style. Others had Old World Bavarian charm. Still others were crude, oblong boxes, the kind used by pioneer undertakers of the Old West.

Further investigation revealed what looked like an oversized vending machine, larger than any vending machine I had ever seen, big enough to fit a body inside. A plate riveted on the back said it was a "Karswell Crematron," patent pending. It smelled like burnt ashes.

"This must be another one of Karswell's inventions," I mused. "One of his 'funeral of the future' ideas.'"

A plate on the front explained how to use it. I gave Dick a synopsis.

"Believe it or not, it's a do-it-yourself cremation machine. You put a body inside, push the button, and viola! All that's left is a cup of the deceased's ashes. This slot here is where you deposit a hundred bucks, which includes California state tax. It prints out six printed copies of the death certificate, too. Those come out of this slot here," I said, pointing to a slit on the side.

Dick called the sheriff, told the deputy what had happened, and to send a couple officers to the Precision Tool Company. He told them where to find it.

An automobile horn sounded outside the building. e should have been at the gate waiting for our ride. We left the two miscreants tied up. They weren't going anywhere. Besides, if the sheriff showed up and found three naked people in the room, we'd be the ones thrown in the clink. Best to return to the lodge. Rochelle could then file charges, fully clothed, at the sheriff's office.

CHAPTER TEN

he deputy's voice grated over the wire: "Listen, lady, if you caught these alleged assailants, why didn't you stay there and wait for us?"

"Because our friend was injured and needed medical attention," I replied, which was partly true. "She had to see the camp nurse right away. She's coming to your office to press charges on the two hoodlums."

"That's just it, lady. What hoodlums? Less than ten minutes after we logged your call we sent two deputies to the Precision Tool Company. The place was empty. We checked every room. Nobody."

"What?"

"You heard me. And if you try this stunt again, you should know you can get into big trouble for filing false reports like this."

"I have two eyewitnesses, besides myself, who can testify those men were there. Either someone helped them escape or they managed to untie themselves."

"That's too bad, lady, because your friend can't press charges now. All we have is your story and no suspects."

I slammed the receiver into its cradle. "Damn!"

Dick had been listening to my end of the conversation.

"What's wrong?"

"The perps got away."

"Just great. This is the second time," Dick griped. "First, when they attacked you, and now Rochelle. Don't you think it's time we had that heart to heart talk you've been putting off? There's something strange going on here, and you're in the thick of it. Rochelle said those lugs thought you two were connected somehow."

"You're right," I confessed. "You deserve to know what's going on. I'm sorry I've kept you in the dark this long, Dick."

We agreed to meet for my confessional at Dick's cabin after dinner. The bloody scrapes on our arms and legs were scabbing up, and still painful. First, I needed a shower and rest.

The jolly crowd in the Mess Hall that evening helped ease the tension around my upcoming "chat" with Dick. Rochelle was back at work, serving meals. The bandages on her shoulders and arms drew sympathetic inquiries from dinner guests. I'd asked her to keep the details to herself, and tell them anything but what really happened. She told them she'd gotten too close to a pot of hot soup on the stove and was burned, which was easy to imagine in an all-nude kitchen.

Dick and I finished our meal of salad, gluten free garlic bread, and Loma Linda meatballs and spaghetti, and were back in his cabin, ready for our heart to heart talk. I sat in the rocking chair and Dick took the Stickley.

"Okay, I'll start this off," Dick announced, "by telling you my full name. I realize we're supposed to use first names only here, but I'm telling you in our new spirit of openness. My name is Dick Barnett of Barnett and Associates Architecture. As for my suspicions about you, it's pretty clear — to me at least — that you're not the average Sunland vacationer. You're here on a mission." Dick's frankness hit the ball squarely into my court. But that's what this gabfest was all about, so, I confessed.

"Okay, here it is: my name is Paloma Liu Tsong of the Confidential Detective Agency in San Francisco. I'm sure you've already guessed I'm half Chinese. 'Paloma' comes from my Spanish mother. And, no, I'm not a secretary, but I suppose you've figured that out too. I'm a private investigator, licensed by the state of California. As for who hired me, you'll have to keep that under your hat; and I mean it! My client is Miss Laura."

Dick's expression told me he was not surprised by what I had just said.

"The Chinese part was obvious," Dick replied. "Your eyes gave you away. You must get your feistiness from the Latin side of your family."

"From both sides," I said. "My Chinese family is just as feisty, if not more so."

"What I'd like to know is," Dick said, "how are you connected to those two creeps at Karswell's lab? I assume the story about you being a contest winner was phony."

"Yes, it was. As for the lederhosen creeps, the first time I ever saw them was in that Solvang parking lot. I still don't know how they knew I would be there.

"Dick, I know this will sound crazy coming from a detective, but I had no idea this was a nudist camp until I got here. I really thought I'd won a contest. Miss Laura sent a letter to my San Francisco office that said I'd won a drawing, and the prize was a free stay here at Sunland. I've never had a vacation, ever. The office was dead, no clients, no cases, so I accepted."

"Paloma, for not knowing you were about to become a nudist, you've adjusted better than 99 percent of our female newbies," Dick said. "You seemed comfortable in the buff as soon as you disrobed."

Dick seemed in such good spirits I thought it was time to make a clean breast of it. No holds barred.

"There's a reason for that, Dick. I've been nude in public before, a lot, in fact. And I'm not talking about a nudist camp. Sunland really is my first nudist camp experience, but before I became a private investigator, I was a Chinatown burlesque queen at Andy Wong's Sky Room. I've danced naked with a giant bubble, with ostrich fans, had a strip tease act, and was part of the Wongettes Showgirl Review. I did two shows, three nights a week."

I braced myself for a lecture on the sordid influence of burlesque on the masses. Instead, he surprised me.

"You're one of the most versatile women I've ever met," he said. "I doubt many nude dancers become licensed private investigators, or know kung fu, can swim like a fish, and even save me from drowning. You've got a wider range of talents than anyone I know, Paloma."

As two people, naked or not, Dick and I had become close, and were getting closer. With my skeletons finally out of the closet, he would make a guilt free sounding board for me on the Karswell case. Of course, he wouldn't know all the answers, but his opinion mattered to me. Like, how did the creeps who jumped me in Solvang end up here at Sunland? And how did they know I wasn't just another nudist?

Dick mulled that over, and replied: "Maybe our famous Hollywood psychic, Jerome Karswell is involved, otherwise why would they be using his lab?"

"Exactly!" I yelped. "It all fits. The Tyrolean hat we found is the same brand Karswell uses in his funeral service; the two men wore lederhosen, used in Karswell's funeral service; the men were in Karswell's secret lab. It all points to that Altadena funeral parlor."

I rocked back and forth in my chair as we brainstormed.

"Dick," I said, "I have another very important question."

"Let's hear it."

"Who puts sun tan oil on *your* back?"

He laughed. "Nobody. I have a gimmick. I fastened a sponge on the end of a back scratcher. It works great."

"I can do better than that." I said. "Come over tomorrow morning for the human touch. I'll put it on for you."

"I look forward to it," he smiled.

I glanced at the Regulator clock on Dick's wall. "Jeez, it's 8:30! I was supposed to call my partner at eight. I forgot to call him last night, too. I'd better get to a phone."

"Your partner?"

"Alexander Blade. I'll bet you know him from the silver screen. He was a kiddie star before moving pictures could talk. Remember the Indian Alley Gang? Well, he was Buster, the kid with the suspenders and oversize cap? After the war, he started his own detective agency. I came on board as his assistant until I became a full partner last year. That's when I got my PI license and ended my dancing career."

"I'm glad we had this talk, Paloma. You seem like a real person now, not just a vague outline. See you in the morning."

"Naked jaybirds couldn't keep me away," I chirped.

It was 8:45 by the time I reached Sunland Lodge. San Francisco General Hospital rules were strict: no patient phone calls after nine o'clock. I slipped into a phone booth, pulled the door shut, and dialed.

"And, operator," I crooned, "please reverse the charges?" Alex wouldn't mind. I was working a case. A familiar voice warbled over the wire.

"Y'ello?"

"Alex! It's Paloma."

"Hang on. Nurse Ilsa is just fluffing my pillow. Now, could you repeat that?"

"PA-LO-MA, remember me? Your partner?"

"That's right! I do have a partner. How's the case, peeper?"

"You will not believe this, Alex, but those same two lederhosen-wearing bozos that strong armed me in Solvang have turned up here at Sunland. They were torturing a sweet kid from our camp inside Karswell's secret laboratory. You remember, Jerome Karswell? The Hollywood psychic?"

"You're right," Alex replied. "It's hard to believe. For one thing, this is the first I've heard about two men in lederhosen. What was that all about?"

"I'm sure I told you, Alex."

"No, Angel Puss, you did not. But let's not argue, this call is going on my hospital bill. Say, why not bring some change when you make these calls?"

"This is a nudist camp, Alex. I'm butt naked. No pockets, no change. And you know what? It's *fantastic*. I can go for a walk in the woods naked, and I don't have to bother with a swimsuit when I go for a swim. There's no more messing around with girdles and garter belts and bras. Nudism has made me realize just how oppressive clothing really is."

"Okay, okay, I get it! You're naked in a phone booth. You're naked in the woods. You're naked in the pool. Keep this up and Nurse Ilsa will have to use the sponge to calm me down. And no, you didn't say a word about being strong armed by two men in lederhosen."

"I didn't? Oh, right, that was — uhm, so, how's the leg?"

"Okay, have it your way, Kitten. Let's forget about the lederhosen. Just give me the dope on the case, fer Pete's sake!"

"Well, I've been here less than a week and there's been a lot of action, but I haven't found the motive behind it yet. For all I know, someone could be blackmailing Karswell. Like I said, today I rescued one of our teenage girls who'd been kidnapped."

"A naked teenage girl kidnapped from a nudist camp? This sounds more like a sleazy paperback novel than a case! What goes on down there, anyway? Oops, hold on! Nurse Ilsa just came back. What? Oh, sure thing, Hon. Will do. Paloma? Nurse Ilsa said the switchboard is about to close down."

I'm in a phone booth butt naked — it's fantastic!

"Okay, I'll have more to report tomorrow."

"I sure hope so. Maybe I'll finally get something for these collect calls. G'night, and don't take any wooden nickels. You've got no place to put 'em. Ha ha."

I hung up and slid out of the booth. Other than a young family playing Monopoly, the lobby was empty. The 20-something wife had her blonde hair tied back in a ponytail. Her husband wore a gold wristwatch. It blazed like the sun, being the only thing he had on. Their young son wore a cowboy hat and gun belt with nickel-plated cap guns.

The evening air was heavy with the scent of pine and oak as I walked back to Jaybird Cottage. An owl hooted in the darkness. When I turned on the sitting room light, my cabin never looked so cozy. I brushed my teeth and slid under the covers of my twin bed. I didn't have to take off complicated undergarments with their snaps and clips, remove make-up, or decide which nightgown to wear. All I had to do was jump into bed. Naked.

CHAPTER 11

he breakfast bell had just banished me from dreamland. That meant Dick would be here any minute. I'd surprise him and be up and out of bed this time. At 7:05 he strode through the door, right on time.

"Did you bring the sun tan oil?" I demanded. "Of course you did. It's behind your back."

He brought out the bottle he was hiding and dropped it in the palm of my hand.

"You know," I began, mimicking his professorial tone, "the sun can be extremely dangerous if you're not prepared for it. Let's see what we can do about that. Turn around."

I began smoothing oil on the back of his neck and across his shoulders, kneading as I went. Down, down, down his back until I reached the dimples above his muscular rear flanks. But I didn't stop there. I continued on down to Mt. Rushmore, waiting for him to flinch. He didn't, so I knelt and I finished his thighs and calves.

"Turn around, Dick," I ordered, and gave him the full frontal sunscreen package. He approved.

"Okay Dick," I said, "and I mean that in every sense of the word; it's your turn."

I gave him the bottle. He poured a generous amount into his palm and rubbed his hands together briskly.

His magic fingers explored every inch of my back, butt, and legs. I spun around. The look on my face dared him to continue. To my surprise, he did! He gave the girls a thorough going over until they stood at attention. He circled my belly button and was headed in the right direction when — well, all I can say is, a girl can't be shy when it comes to sun safety. He squeezed and squeezed until he got every last drop out of that bottle. I was as limp as grilled cheese.

"Breakfast?" Dick said when he had finished. "I'm starved."

"Me too," I gurgled.

Safely cocooned within our glistening layer of sun tan oil, we strolled to the Mess Hall.

Naturally, we discussed the case over breakfast. It was time to take charge, I said; maybe even venture into the valley of the textiles. That would mean suiting up, hiding our beloved nakedness. Convincing Dick to leave Sunland might be a challenge, but I had a feeling he would go along.

We split up after breakfast. Dick had to take care of camp business, and I went to the lodge to inform Miss Laura of my plans. Given the perps' mysterious knowledge of our personal affairs, Miss Laura's fear that someone was listening in was well founded. I thought it best we talk outside.

I approached the front desk. "Miss Laura, would you step outside for a minute? This won't take long."

Borealis got up from her roll-top desk where she had been going over paperwork. We walked across the front porch, down the stairs, and stopped at a safe distance from the lodge.

I faced her and said: "Would you arrange a meeting with your husband for me? But first, I want to check out his Altadena funeral parlor. I plan to assume the role of a grieving niece in need of funeral arrangements for my uncle. I'm sure I can talk Dick into playing the part of my husband. My hunch is, the two men who kidnapped Rochelle are working in that parlor. Then I'd like to talk to Jerome, if you can arrange it for me."

"That won't be a problem," she said, "Do you suspect something's going on here at the lodge? Is that why you brought me all the way out here?"

"Yes, I do. I believe your intuition was correct. Someone knows everything about us, things that could only be learned by a tapped phone or hidden microphone. Your office may be the source of the leak. As soon as I finish my work in Altadena, we'll go through the office with a fine tooth comb."

"In that case," Borealis sputtered, "I'll use our public phones for calling out, and I certainly won't share privileged information while I'm in the office. Let's go back inside, I have something for you."

We returned to her office, where Borealis picked up a pencil and began scribbling words on a notepad. She crossed the room to a weather-beaten armoire, where she rummaged for a few items. She handed the note to me, along with the items. The note said: "Take this hat and veil to cover your face. Give Dick these sunglasses. No one will recognize you with clothes on anyway. And BE CAREFUL!"

Miss Laura's warning in all caps was good advice. I had no idea what we might find. Returning to Jaybird Cottage, I opened the suitcase Dick told me no self respecting nudist would need to open. Good thing I'd packed my dark blue Vera Maxwell suit for special occasions. The jacket

Karswell Chapel of the Chimes, Altadena, California

flared at the hips and the skirt fell just below my knees. It would cover nicely, though after a week without textiles it would be difficult to wear them again. I went to the oak dresser and pulled out my panty girdle, nylons, and Permalift bra.

Then, Dick walked in. He looked perplexed when he saw the open suitcase on my bed.

"What gives with the textiles, kid? You look like you're about to suit up."

"We are."

"We are?"

"Yes. As of today we're a happily married couple, and I've just lost my dear uncle Wolfgang. We're going to Karswell's Bavarian funeral parlor to make arrangements for his funeral. I hope you're up for some detective work."

I gave Dick the lowdown. He agreed to the plan, even if it meant suiting up. On the day he checked into Sunland for his vacation he was wearing his office outfit. That look would be perfect.

Within an hour, we emerged from our cabins like two caterpillars that had turned into textile butterflies. We were a typical Los Angeles couple. Well, almost. Dick said we should leave the Rambler and take his Pontiac convertible. We made one last stop at the lodge to ask Miss Laura to call Gatekeeper. He would have to unlock the gate to let us out.

Twenty minutes later, Gatekeeper met us at the gate looking somewhat amused.

"I hardly recognized you!" he chuckled.

"Thanks," Dick replied. "That's exactly what we want."

"Will you be coming back?"

"You bet we will," I replied. "We'll be back."

Gatekeeper waved us through the open gate and we headed down the mountain road. It was a short drive to Altadena once we reached the 210 Highway. In less than an hour we were exiting on North Arroyo into Pasadena. I had never traveled this far south, so this was all new to me, but Dick lived here. He knew where he was going.

We turned onto West Woodbury Road, then North Marengo, heading into Altadena. Karswell's funeral parlor loomed on the corner of Ventura and La Fiesta, facing Mountain View Cemetery.

The Chapel of the Chimes stood out like a Bavarian boil on an otherwise normal looking block of shops and restaurants. Obviously, this was Karswell's intention. The façade resembled a medieval, half-timbered building in the Miltenberg style. Dick, the architect, told me all about it.

"The Germans call this style Bauernhaus," he droned. "It's a variation on Bavarian farm house designs. The half-timbered facades give these buildings their distinctive look."

"If there's a Bavarian gunsel inside this Bauernhaus," I growled, "he's all mine."

"Now, now, Honey Bunch," Dick cautioned, "you're mourning the loss of dear uncle Wolfgang, remember?" "You've got to stay in character."

"Yes, you're right," I said. "I can do it."

Entering the parlor lobby, I felt as though I had stepped onto the movie set for The Bride of Frankenstein. Somewhere in the room, a hidden speaker wheezed a German accordion tune, barely audible and very discrete.

We must have activated an invisible beam when we entered the parlor, because a straw-haired blonde in her early 20s magically appeared in the room. She wore her hair in braids. Her dress, a Bavarian *dirndl* with pink and gold threads, shimmered as she walked, while her low-cut neckline revealed Alpine cleavage. An apron of transparent tulle glistened with pearl embroidery. She oozed sex appeal and Aryan perfection, if blue-eyed Aryan babes are your thing.

"*Guten tag*!" The *fraulein* twittered. "I am Ava. May I help you?" Her dainty fingers flicked a golden braid off her shoulder.

Dick explained the reason for our visit as I dabbed a hanky behind my Raybans.

"My wife's uncle Wolfgang recently moved on to his new life in Valhalla. We want him to have the kind of funeral he would have had back in the Old Country. Understand?"

"Oh, yah," the busty blonde exclaimed. "I understand perfectly. That is our mission. We may live in Los Angeles, California, but within these walls we are back home. That is our specialty, Herr…?"

"Nachtmann," Dick said. "Frederik Nachtmann. And this is my bereaved wife Greta." At that, he clicked his heels together, picked up the bimbo's hand, and daintily planted his lips on the back of it. Her eyelashes fluttered over big, blue peepers that drank in every inch of the masculine hunk in front of her. It didn't take a mind reader to see she approved. Oh, yah.

"Herr Nachtmann," the sun kissed fraulein warbled. "have you heard of our Oktoberfest Farewell service?"

"That's exactly why we're here!" Dick exclaimed. "We'd like to learn more about it."

"*Wunderbar*!" she yelped in feminine approval. "Please, follow me into the gallery."

Her hips rolled side to side seductively under her dirndl as she lead us to a large room of caskets, flower arrangements, stained glass, and candelabras. Maybe it was my imagination, but the accordion music seemed louder here. She stopped in front of an imposing casket made of steel plate, held together with rivets. It resembled the hull of the Titanic.

"This," she recited, "is our 'Fearless Leader.' It is made of stainless steel, with reinforced sides, bottom, and lid. It has a pleated lining made of the softest satin. The underside of the lid, as you can see," she moved her well-manicured fingers in a sweeping motion under the lid, "is lined with the finest California redwood. Your uncle would be so proud of a casket as fine as this."

Finally, I broke into the conversation. "Yes, he would," I said. "Uncle Wolfgang loved redwood trees. Especially tall ones."

The blonde bimbo looked at me as if I'd suddenly appeared out of nowhere, then turned back to Dick to finish her spiel.

"Included in the Oktoberfest Farewell package is an authentic Bavarian band that will play at the reception after your uncle's service.

She wore braids and a lowcut neckline that revealed Alpine cleavage.

But first, you must choose which *tracht* your uncle will wear. The most popular for men is lederhosen.

"Our lederhosen comes in several types of leather, but buckskin is most frequently ordered because of its softness. We also have cowhide, wild boar hide, and goatskin. One important detail is the button-down flap or 'bib' over the fly. All our lederhosen flies are embroidered with traditional designs by Old World artisans. In terms of the length of your uncle's lederhosen, we have short, medium, and long. The short length stops mid-thigh; the Knickerbocker is mid-length and stops just above the knee. Our full-length version reaches to the ankles.

"Now for the shoes. The Oktoberfest Farewell includes a pair of *Haferlschuhs*. That's a leather half-boot with a sturdy sole and a characteristic tongue over the instep that I am sure you're familiar with."

"Of course," I said, having no idea what she was talking about.

"As for the shirt and jacket," she prattled, "the *Pfoad* is the most traditional. It's a pullover, and opens down to the midriff. The buttons are Bavarian, made with a choice of antler horn, leather, or embossed metal. The typical Bavarian shirt is made of linen or combed cotton, and can be checkered, white, or plain, natural shades. Collars are standard turnovers or stand-up; we also offer a button-down collar. On the other hand, if you want a more formal look, you might consider a traditional *Janker*. We offer a *loden* blazer or a more casual knitted cardigan. Loden is a type of broadcloth, and it's wind and waterproof. Any questions so far?"

Dick turned to me. "I hope you're taking notes, dear," he said. "I got lost somewhere around the embroidered fly." Before I could reply, the fraulein came yodeling to his rescue.

"Don't worry, Herr Nachtmann!" she smiled. "We don't expect you to remember all these details. I have an Oktoberfest Farewell brochure that contains everything we've discussed. There's a checklist on the back, so you can mark which features you wish to include in your package. Simply return it to me when you're finished."

I gave Dick a knowing nudge when the blonde wasn't looking.

"I have a question," I said. "How will my uncle be transported to his final resting place?"

"I'm glad you asked!" the trollop gushed. "He will travel in our custom-built Mercedes hearse, driven by our two hearsemen, who keep it polished and maintained. Would you like to see it?"

"I would, indeed," I said.

"Walk this way, please," she said. Her hips jiggled this way and that as we jiggled along behind her.

The double doors at the rear of the gallery opened into a spacious garage. Stacked from floor to ceiling were various models of caskets. Two men wearing lederhosen were working on a black Mercedes hearse. One was polishing the front fenders while the other cleaned the side windows, which had crossed palm leaves under a German eagle etched into the glass.

"The windows and doors of this hearse are bulletproof for ultimate safety," the Tyrolean trollop explained. Pointing at the two men, she added, "That is Johann on the left, and Herman on the right. It will be their responsibility to transport your uncle with utmost care to his final resting place." She hauled her caboose to the hearse and spoke something to the men. They turned and waved at us.

I may not know Johann and Herman by name, but I knew their ugly mugs. They were the ones who attacked me and kidnapped Rochelle. I'd brought my Argus camera just for this moment. I poked Dick in the side with my elbow.

"It's them," I whispered. "I'm going to get a picture, but I want them to think I'm taking it of you and the bimbo. Wait till she comes back!"

Dick held onto my arm. "Okay sweetness," he whispered. "You set it up."

The undulating edelweiss returned, smiling.

I asked her: "Would you mind if I took a snapshot of you and my husband with my uncle's hearse in the background? I'd like to show it to my aunt. She was too despondent to come with us today."

I knew she wouldn't refuse.

"Yes, I think that would be fine," she said, and sidled up as close to Dick as Santa Claus to Christmas, her arm hooked in his. I made sure the yokels next to the hearse were watching when I fired off two shots.

"That's wonderful, thank you," I said. "You should be a model."

"Well, when I'm not here I do a little fashion modeling in Hollywood. Shall we go into the office to discuss the details of your uncle's Oktoberfest Farewell?"

"Definitely," Dick said. "But we have an appointment with her uncle's attorney at two o'clock, and we're running late." Dick nodded in my direction. "Once we hear the details of Uncle Wolfgang's will, we will return to finalize the service. We're looking forward to it."

Dick poured on the charm, took her hand and smooched it a second time. What a hambo.

Back in Dick's Pontiac, we sorted things out as he drove us back to Sunland. Crossing the Colorado Street Bridge was quite an experience for someone like me who'd never seen it before.

"Remind me not to have accordion music at my funeral," I said. "Can you believe that Oktoberfest Farewell package? Still, you have to marvel at the mind that came up with it. I think it's time I met The Incredible Karswell. Tomorrow if possible."

CHAPTER 12

he orange and black Angels Flight railcar came to a stop at the end of the line on Hill Street. I'd never ridden Angels Flight, only seen it in movies, so I thought I'd spend a nickel and travel in style. After all, I was still on vacation.

The car was oddly shaped, built on a rakish slant for climbing the steep hill. Stepping aboard, I steadied myself by holding on to iron poles spaced along the center walkway until I reached the high end of the car. Bench seats ran the entire length of both sides of the car, and I claimed my seat at the very top. The car even had a name: *Olivet*, and it filled with passengers within a few minutes. An air horn sounded, followed by a clanking and whirring of moving cables as we began to climb. I watched a steady stream of autos disappear into the Third Street Tunnel below. Halfway uphill we passed *Sinai*, *Olivet*'s identical twin on its way down. The cars passed within a hair's breath of one another. It seemed like the trip had just begun when we jerked to a stop at the Olive Street station. I was the first passenger to disembark, and began my walk down Olive Street.

The Karswell Arms was a shabby hotel that did its best to lower the value of real estate on the 200 block of Olive Street. I remembered Dick telling me how Bunker Hill was slated for the wrecking ball, and from the look of the Karswell Arms, it wouldn't take much to knock it down. Miss Laura had called ahead, informing Karswell of my visit. He was none too pleased, she said, but reluctantly agreed to meet me if I kept our talk on the QT. He was, after all, a Hollywood personality with an image to uphold. Not one word about his missing coffin should reach the gossip rags, he said.

After climbing three steps to the portico, I read names on the mailboxes, each with its own button. I pushed number 9, under KARSWELL.

A voice crackled over the speaker.

"Yes?"

"Paloma Liu Tsong to see Mr. Karswell," I said. Silence followed, then a loud buzz that unlocked the front door. I entered. The buzzing continued as I made my way through the musty lobby to a corridor on my right. A sign pointing down the hall said: "Apartments 1–10."

I rapped my knuckles on the door until it swung open, and there he was: The Incredible Karswell, looking like a lovesick pudding doll with a case of the DTs. In his haste to reach the door, he'd forgotten to tie his pink satin kimono. It gaped open. His potbelly hung over boxer shorts festooned with tropical plants and pineapples. He looked like a two-legged fruit cocktail. His famous snow-white spit curl clung damply to his forehead. Nevertheless, he maintained a stately aura about him, as if he were a member of the Roman senate descending from on high to greet "the people."

"Well? Don't just stand there gawking," he gargled. His eyes narrowed as he took a closer look at me. "I hope you're not one of those Maoists who believes in the little Red Book."

"If you're asking if I'm a Communist, no, I'm not. I'm Chinese American, born and raised in California."

"I wouldn't want my wife working with a Commie," he blathered. "They can't be trusted. They'll use any means necessary to destroy what America stands for. The end justifies their means."

"May I come in?"

He bowed and swept his hand before him in a theatrical gesture of welcome. I entered.

Karswell bade me sit on an ancient camel back sofa, upholstered in red mohair that a starved moth wouldn't touch. It felt like it was stuffed with baseballs. Hand carved gargoyles leered out from the armrests. I remarked on its Victorian design, making empty conversation, when suddenly, his mood brightened.

"This sofa is quite special," Karswell intoned like a delirious bass fiddle. "It was given to me by William Randolph Hearst. But — its original owner was Lionel Barrymore. Bill and Lionel were close friends, you know."

I didn't bother to ask how Hearst ended up with Lionel Barrymore's sofa or why Hearst would want Karswell to have it.

Posters from Karswell's performances embellished the walls. Framed photographs of Karswell himself hung in every available space. The photos showed him beaming as he posed with Hollywood celebrities like Joan Crawford and Mae West. I saw only one photo of his wife. She appeared in a scene from a Shakespeare play: Ophelia to Karswell's Hamlet in their halcyon days of the theater.

Karswell also collected fortunetelling paraphernalia. He had a crystal ball, a substantial library of occult books, tarot card decks, a replica of an Egyptian sarcophagus, and — his coffin! Framed by an arch leading into the next room, it rested on a custom built platform.

"May I get you some coffee, tea, absinthe perhaps?" Karswell queried.

"No, thank you," I said. "But, that coffin over there; I was led to believe it was missing. I mean, that's why your wife hired me, to find it."

Maybe it was just an act, or a way to get rid of me, but Karswell downplayed its mysterious reappearance.

"You might say my wife jumped the gun," he said. "The search is over. A Good Samaritan returned it last night. It was all a misunderstanding, nothing more."

"What do you mean by 'misunderstanding?'"

"The shop owner sent it to the wrong address, pure and simple. Once the Good Samaritan discovered it belonged to me, he returned it."

"According to your wife, the shop owner filed a police report when he discovered it missing."

"I know nothing about that," he scoffed. "As you can see, there it sits."

This was all too curious. I wanted to know more.

"I've heard so much about your grandfather's coffin. May I take a closer look?"

"I'll give you the Karswell guided tour!" he bellowed, and launched himself off the Barrymore sofa. He grabbed the martini glass that sat on an end table. It was half empty, or half full, if you're Karswell.

"Follow me," he slurped.

The casket looked as though it was built for an extra wide person. According to Miss Laura, it needed the extra room to hold grandfather Karswell's lifesaving gadgetry as well as himself.

The Incredible Karswell began his tour.

"Grandfather called it the Omega III, 'For the discerning customer who isn't sure he's quite dead.' You see, Miss Liu, grandfather was something of a seer, in his own way. He knew that deep down inside us all, we know that — whether we admit it or not — one day the Grim Reaper will come calling. Dying is as natural as being born, but unlike birth, death has a PR problem. Most of us cannot admit we're going to die. In fact, some people become quite desperate when confronted with the reality of their immanent demise. They will do almost anything to forestall the inevitable. In grandfather Karswell's case, he hedged his bets with the Omega III.

"Although he realized he would lose in the end, he just could not imagine himself dead. You see, one imagines one's impending doom is a mistake somehow, a misdiagnosis perhaps. All one needs is an operation, a miracle pill, a trip to Lourdes, perhaps, to bounce right back. In some rare cases, one may appear dead to those around him, but, alas, is not. Remember Poe's *The Premature Burial*? That story had a profound effect on grandfather Karswell, I'm afraid.

"Anyway, as I was saying, the Omega III was designed for the person who doubts his own death. It comes stocked with the loved one's favorite snack foods, water to last a week, a copy of the *Gideon Bible*, batteries to run a one-watt light bulb — you'd be surprised how bright one watt can be when you're sealed inside a coffin — and a radiophone to call the nearest police station for a rescue unit. The Omega III has everything one would need to weather an entire week of premature burial, the 'faux death,' as grandfather called it."

I said: "Your wife did mention your grandfather's fear of premature burial."

"Oh, it was much more than that, my friend," Karswell crooned. "It became his inspiration, his purpose in life. He created a business enterprise out of his greatest fear. Can you imagine that? He was a true inspiration to the Karswell clan."

"He must have been disappointed when he knew his time had finally come."

"Yes, he knew the inevitable was coming. And yet he couldn't imagine a world without him in it. We are all in denial when it comes time to face our departure from this world, wouldn't you say, Miss Liu?"

"I wouldn't know. Ask me when I'm not on vacation."

"Exactly! I rest my case. But, back to the Omega III," Karswell blathered. "It has plenty of room as you can see. I added a few amenities after grandfather died, like the cigarette dispenser in a pocket on the left side. Naturally, I installed a No Smoking sign that comes on once the lid is sealed. It dispenses my favorite cigarette — Krakatoa Kretek — a clove-infused Indonesian brand. Here, I'll show you how it works."

With deft motions, his fingers felt along the satin interior until they found a slit in the lining. He pushed a button. Out popped a single cigarette, which Karswell quickly snapped up.

"You see?" he said, holding the cigarette between his thumb and forefinger. That's when a frown creased his smooth-as-marble map.

"That's odd."

"What's wrong?" I asked.

"This cigarette," he said, staring intently. "It's a Lucky Strike, not my brand, not even close! What is this? Where did this come from?"

"Maybe you should take a closer look, Mr. Karswell. Is this the right coffin?"

"It must be! Let's see, the martini dispenser I installed should be over here."

His hands fumbled frantically, feeling here and there.

"It's not here! That's not possible."

He dug deeper into the coffin's innards. From his frantic expression, I knew he had found more problems.

"You're right, Miss Liu! This isn't grandfather Karswell's coffin!" he squalled. "It's an imposter!"

CHAPTER 13

lutching his martini, Karswell collapsed onto Lionel Barrymore's sofa like a wilted pink flower. He looked catatonic. Then, slowly he plucked the olive from the martini glass. His even, white teeth gripped the pimiento-stuffed olive, removed it from its toothpick, and began chewing.

"Consider yourself back on the case, Miss Liu," he groaned.

I tried pulling him out of his funk by changing the subject.

"You must have inherited your gift of invention from your grandfather."

It took awhile for my words to break through the cloud of mental smog that smothered him.

"Huh? What? Oh, actually, no. It was my father, Clarence Karswell, grandfather's only child. We Karswell's do have the gift. I suppose dad inherited his from grandfather. He was a well-known scientist and metaphysician here in Los Angeles. The mortuary was merely a part time affair for grandfather. Occult science was his true calling. He founded a group of like-minded individuals for experimental research projects.

"You wouldn't know this, Miss Liu, but grandfather was one of the first flying saucer contactees. In fact, he wrote a book about the time he rode in a flying saucer. The alien beings invited him aboard their craft. As a child, I would sit on his knee and listen to his tales about the little green men from Planet Floot. That's what he called it, Planet Floot. I have no idea what the aliens called it. Marvelous stories for a youngster like myself. Marvelous!"

"How interesting, Mr. Karswell, but I need to tell you about something that happened at Sunland recently. Did you know that two of your funeral home employees kidnapped one of your Sunland guests and held her prisoner at the Precision Tools warehouse?"

"What? Two of my employees?" he rasped.

"We caught them in your laboratory above Karswell Falls. You do have a warehouse up there, don't you?"

"Of course I do," he barked, regaining his dour demeanor.

I must have hit a nerve. The lab was supposed to be top secret.

"It's where research and development for Karswell Funeral Parlors Incorporated take place. I don't allow anyone up there unless I'm present. Too many hush-hush projects there to allow unsupervised visitors."

"In that case, you'd better change the locks," I said. "Someone's been using it. The men I saw are employed at your Altadena funeral parlor as hearse drivers."

"I don't hire employees, oh, no, no, no. That's Brace Moreland's job. He manages day-to-day operations. I have my personal appearances, books, lectures, and my private practice to keep up. I consult for many Hollywood stars, as you know."

"I understand. When was the last time you used the lab?"

"It has been awhile," Karswell mused. He stroked his chin, staring at the floor. "I'd say, six months ago. I locked the doors last March."

"And you've given no one permission to use it?"

"Of course not, but now that you've told me this, I'm going to send Brace Moreland up there to have a look around."

"If Brace Moreland is in charge, maybe he sent those men up there."

"I can't imagine that...well...in any case, Miss Liu, I appreciate this little chat of ours, disturbing as it was. But now I must prepare for my book signing at the Santa Monica pier. It's for my latest book, *Amnesia In Colonial America*. I lecture at the pier every month by special arrangement."

That was my cue to buzz off. I thanked him for his time and Karswell waved me off at the door. It was late afternoon, and the sidewalk along Olive Street radiated heat from a blazing August sun. It made me even more uncomfortable inside my layers of clothing.

Before climbing aboard Angels Flight for my return to Hill Street, I stopped at the Angels Flight Pharmacy to make a phone call. I found the phone booth and dialed Laura Borealis, using the number of one of the lobby phones at the lodge. If she was anywhere near that phone, she'd pick up; she was and she did.

"Sunland Lodge!"

"Miss Laura, it's Paloma. What was the name of the shop that reupholstered Jerome's coffin?"

"Altadena Upholstery," she said. "It's just around the corner from the funeral parlor."

"Thanks, I'll report in later. First, I want to talk to that upholstery shop owner."

• • •

I jockied the Rambler into a tight space between a late model Cadillac and a Hudson Commodore sedan parked on La Fiesta, and walked the rest of the way to the upholstery shop. The man behind the counter was tying down coil springs on a love seat. It could have been the owner, but I didn't ask. He glanced up through tired eyes when I walked in.

"May I help you, Miss?"

"I hope so." I pulled out my wallet, showed him my PI photostat, and he looked impressed.

"Oh, a detective! What can I do for you?"

"I was hired to find Jerome Karswell's missing coffin," I explained. "But I'm happy to report it's been returned to Mr. Karswell's apartment."

"Fantastic!' the man exclaimed. "I was real upset when it disappeared. As a small business owner, that's the kind of thing that keeps you up at night. You know how people are. Customers might think twice about leaving their furniture here, like maybe they think they won't get it back. I don't mind telling you, this takes a load off my mind."

"I heard the coffin got sent to the wrong address."

"Not on our life, young lady!" the upholsterer protested. "We never make mistakes like that. We make sure every piece goes to its rightful owner. I opened the shop one morning and, poof, the coffin was gone. Somebody jimmied the back door. That's how they got in, through the back door. The police came, I filed a report, and that was that. I haven't heard a peep about it since, not until you told me. In any case, I'm relieved to know it's been returned."

"In that case, I'm happy to be the bearer of such good news." I said. "Thanks for your time."

As I walked back to my car I wondered why someone would bother to palm off a counterfeit coffin on The Incredible Karswell? What happened to the real one, and who was the so-called "Good Samaritan" that made the switch?

From Altadena, I drove to the *Los Angeles Times* on the corner of Broadway and First, in downtown LA. I hoped to talk to their crime reporter.

I told the receptionist the purpose of my visit. She had a tan complexion and blonde hair, a common sight in Los Angeles.

"You'll want to see Peggy Marshall," she squeaked. "She's got the crime beat. The newsroom is up those stairs. I'll let her know you're coming."

She picked up her desk phone and dialed Marshall's number. After a brief conversation, she hung up and sent me to the stairway.

"She's at the desk next to the water cooler," the receptionist said. I began climbing.

I'd seen Marshall's byline in the *Times*. Sunland guests can pick up fresh copies of the *Times* at the lodge every morning. Since Karswell is a household name in Hollywood, Marshall should know a thing or two about him, but I hoped she could identify the two men from the funeral parlor.

I saw the water cooler at the far side of the newsroom and sauntered in that direction. Peggy Marshall was waiting for me. She stood up and waved to guide me in.

"Miss Liu?" she greeted.

"Yes, thanks for taking the time to see me."

"How can I help you?"

I explained that I'd come from San Francisco to work on a case involving The Incredible Karswell. I also told her about the skirmish I'd had in Solvang and again with the same two men at Precision Tool Company.

"Since you've got the crime beat," I said, "I was hoping you might recognize the two men. I've got a photo."

"I can try. Let's see it."

Marshall looked at the photo.

"Sorry, I can't say that I do," she said. "But it's funny you should mention Karswell. Lately I've been covering a series of fortuneteller murders."

"Yes, I've read one of your stories about that a couple days ago," I said. "The Crystal Ball Killer?"

"Yes, that's what I call him, but so far, I can't determine a motive for these murders, and neither can the cops. He's killed three in the last two weeks.

"His trademark is odd, too. He smashes the murdered fortuneteller's crystal ball. Even more bizarre are the letters he's sent to me; rambling rants taunting the LAPD to stop him. The case is shaping up to be bigger than the Black Dahlia murder."

"We may have something in common," I said. "We're both working on cases that have to do with fortunetellers, even though Karswell doesn't consider himself one, nor does he like the term psychic. He prefers 'forecaster.'"

"I suppose we do have something in common," Marshall replied. "In any case, the LAPD is up against the wall on these murders, even having one eyewitness. I interviewed him for the morning edition. He saw a strange figure coming out of the last murder victim's apartment. But here's the weird part: the killer wore a black executioner's hood and a black robe with a white circle and a cross hairs in the center. Even in LA it's not every day you see someone dressed like that. Maybe for a Halloween party, but that's it."

"Odd," I replied. "Karswell didn't mention these fortuneteller murders when we talked this morning. I guess he was more upset someone had replaced his granddad's coffin with a coffin that wasn't his."

Marshall replied: "I've heard how Karswell likes to sleep in that coffin. But why would someone bother pulling a switch like that? Holding it for ransom maybe?"

"Dunno," I said. "Makes no sense to me, either. He wants it kept under wraps for now, so that's off the record."

"Seems we're on a similar path," Marshall said. "In my case, other than the victims being fortunetellers, I'm hard-pressed to get into the killer's head. There's a law on the books that bans fortunetellers in Los Angeles County. It hasn't been enforced since before the war, but there's a group of local citizens that's been pressuring the DA to run fortunetellers out of town."

"So you think someone's taken the law into their own hands?" I asked. "Maybe one of the concerned citizens has gone rogue?"

"I've considered that angle," Marshall said. "Until more facts turn up, it's a stretch. I think we should keep in touch, Miss Liu. As for Karswell's coffin, I wouldn't be surprised if it wasn't just one of his publicity stunts."

"If we're collaborating, call me Paloma."

"Okay, Paloma. If I need to get in touch with you, where are you staying?"

"I'm at Sunland Vacation Camp near Tujunga. The only phones we have are two public phone booths at the lodge. If our camp administrator, Laura Borealis picks up, leave a message with her."

Marshall raised her eyebrows and gave me a sly look. "Sunland's a nudist colony. You're a nudist, then?"

"I am now. It's my first nudist camp experience."

"Is Sunland a hotbed of sex and Socialism like the tabloids claim?"

"I've seen a few sunburned backsides," I said, "but other than that, I haven't met any Reds. I have to admit I enjoy the freedom. I know it might sound weird, but it feels great being outdoors stark naked."

That's when Peggy Marshall surprised me. "Not weird at all," she confessed. "After being cooped up in this office all week, I get the urge to feel a little free myself. An overall tan is one of my summertime goals every year. There's a secluded nude beach up the Pacific Coast Highway above Malibu. I go there nearly every weekend during the warm weather months, which are quite a few here."

We exchanged phone numbers and agreed to call if we something important came up. I left the Times building and drove into the thick of downtown LA, a world of concrete, steel, glass, and autos. I stopped at Clifton's cafeteria for lunch.

If you've never been to Clifton's Cafeteria, it's quite an experience. The vast interior looks like a forest, with fake rocks, running streams, artificial trees, and meandering paths.

Moving down the cafeteria line, I chose the Catalina Tuna salad sandwich and a bowl of stained glass Jell-O for dessert. I carried my tray to a table next to a cascading waterfall, where I listened to the water and ate my sandwich. A towering redwood soared to the second story ceiling in the center of the dining room.

I felt more confused about the Karswell case than I was before I met Peggy Marshall, and downtown LA was far too noisy to gather my thoughts. I finished my meal and drove back to Sunland.

They were listening to every word in Miss Laura's office.

CHAPTER 14

While waiting for Gatekeeper to let me in, I finished a crossword puzzle, filed my nails, and sang along with Patti Page who warbled, *Would I Love You, Love You, Love You* on the car radio. He finally ambled down the dirt road, key ring in hand. He moved like a snail with a bum leg, but made up for his lack of speed with a cheery personality.

"Welcome back, Missy! How was your trip into the valley of the textiles?"

"Too confining," I cafetched. "I'm ready to frolic naked under the pines."

"Well, before you start frolicking, you might want to check in with Miss Laura," he advised. "She left word she wants to see you."

"I'll do that, thanks."

As I shifted the Rambler into gear, Gatekeeper yelped: "Hold on a minute, Missy! Here's that license number you wanted. I wrote it down the other day. Forgot to give it to you."

I thanked Gatekeeper for remembering and drove off. A thick plume of dust trailed behind the Rambler as I dodged several familiar but deadly potholes along the way.

At Sunland Lodge, I pulled up next to a Model A Ford pick-up used by the maintenance crew. I was cocooned in my street clothes, but did not want to keep Miss Laura waiting while I stripped at my cabin. Now that I was a full fledged camp member I felt like a traitor for wearing them.

"Ah, Miss Paloma," Laura Borealis greeted as she dusted off the lobby TV set. "How was Jerome? Respectful for a change, I hope?"

"Yes, he was," I said. "He even offered tea."

"But was he helpful?"

"Yes and no," I replied. "Long story short, I found his coffin in your apartment."

Borealis yelped: "What? How can that be?"

"Your husband said its disappearance was a mistake; that the upholstery shop sent it to the wrong address. However, you should know that I did speak with the owner of the shop. He advised that the coffin did indeed disappear as you said. He confirmed his shop had been broken into. He filed a police report."

With a tinge of anger, Borealis replied: "Why would Jerome lie about something like this?"

"I'm not sure he was lying, Miss Laura. He was lied to. He said a 'Good Samaritan' returned the coffin. However, while he was demonstrating the coffin's new features, he found out it was a clever fake. Whoever made it missed a few details, and your husband found certain components missing."

"But who would do such a thing, and why?"

"That's the big question. Now, what was it you wanted to see me about?"

"Let's step onto the front porch for a moment, dear," she said.

We walked through the front doors onto the front porch.

"I think you were right about my office," she whispered. "I mean, about there being a leak. It didn't register with me until you brought it up, but lately I've noticed an odd clicking sound on the office phone. If my memory serves me, it began around the time you arrived, possibly a week before."

"It would explain a few things I've been wondering about," I said. "I'd be happy to search the office for bugs if you'd like."

"Would you? I don't mind telling you I've got the screaming meemies."

"First, I've got to get rid of these clothes," I groaned. "Then I'll speak with Dick about giving us a hand."

I returned to Jaybird Cottage and stripped to bare skin. When the girdle came off I felt ten pounds lighter. I put on my cartwheel hat, sandals, and Chinese jade necklace and went outside to search for Mr. Barnett. After checking the pool and the library without luck, I finally cornered him in the Rec Hall, repairing the microphone on the stage's podium.

"Paloma! How'd it go with Karswell?"

"I made some progress I'll tell you about later, but right now we've got a job to do. Miss Laura needs our help. She's convinced her office is bugged. Want to find out?"

"Sounds like more fun than what I'm doing here."

We left the hall for the lodge, where Laura was discussing next week's menu with Naked Chef.

"Don't mind us," I said as we entered the office.

She wrapped her up her conversation with Naked Chef and reclined in her easy chair to watch the hunt. Her phone was an obvious choice, and an easy one, so we saved that for last. We examined walls, chairs, the water cooler, the moose head, potted plants, paintings and the framed photographs on the walls.

I found our first bug behind a Paint-By-Numbers rendering of a tropical island. A tiny microphone stuck to the wall had been listening to every word spoken in Miss Laura's office. It had no wires attached, something I'd never seen before. I pried it loose with my fingernail and showed it to Dick. He took a magnifying glass from Miss Laura's desk.

"It has some lettering," Dick said. He moved the glass closer, then farther away to bring it into focus. I put a finger to my lips to shush him. Picking up a note pad and pencil I wrote: "Don't talk, write!" I shoved the pad and pencil into his hand.

In all caps, he scribbled:

"ACME TOY CO. PASADENA, CALIFORNIA."

I took back the notepad and wrote: "Would a toy company bug a nudist camp?"

A Paint by Numbers tropic isle hid a small, round microphone.

Dick put his lips close to my ear, cupping his hands. He whispered:

"I'd like to show this to a friend of mine at Caltech. He can tell us all about this thing."

That would mean suiting up again! I still had girdle marks on my thighs from the last trip. Then I remembered the license number Gatekeeper had given me. Whispering in Dick's ear, I said:

"Gatekeeper got the license of the car with the two thugs in it. Before we go to Caltech, I'll give the number to my partner. His DMV contact will trace it."

I hurried to a lobby phone booth where I dialed San Francisco General and waited for the switchboard to pick up. The operator connected me to Room 217 where, as luck would have it, Alex was between sponge baths.

"Y'ello?"

"Things are hotting up on the case, Alex," I said with an upbeat lilt in my voice.

"Really? Is this a collect call because you're naked and have no pockets?"

"Ha ha, no. I borrowed some nickels from Miss Laura. If your buddy at DMV will run a California plate number for me chop chop, it might give me a big break in the case, Alex."

"Why not? It's been pretty boring knitting my broken leg back together. And it's Nurse Ilsa's day off. That means I get her useless wannabe, Clara Dishwater. Believe me, you do not want a sponge bath from Cara Dishwater. She doesn't know one end of a sponge from the other. Where's my damn pencil? Hang on, I think it's on the nightstand."

I listened to the rustling sound of sheets, then a crash of metal on the floor.

"Damn! There goes my water tray!" Alex cursed. "I'll call nurse Clara when I get off the blower. Okay, give me the number."

"MSB557."

"Got it. First, the nurse, then DMV. My contact will get results pronto, don't you worry. Give me your number there."

"It's a public phone here in the lobby," I said. "Just keep ringing if I don't pick up right away."

I recited the number and Alex scribbled it across his bowel movements chart.

"Yeah, yeah, got it. 'K, talk to you later!"

Click.

Back in the office, Dick continued his debugging crusade, unscrewing the base of Miss Laura's desk phone.

"It's my last stop on this egg hunt," Dick said. "And, viola!"

He found another tiny microphone, exactly like the one behind the painting. He wrapped them both in several Kleenex tissues and put them into an empty cigar box he retrieved from the waste basket. For good measure, he sealed the lid with tape he found on Miss Laura's desk.

"That should keep them out of trouble," Dick said. "Anyway, I think this is the last of them."

I said to Borealis: "You were right. Someone's been listening to everything that went on in this office. It explains the two yeggs that roughed me up in Solvang, too. They knew I was coming and probably tailed me."

As we pondered the extent of the camp's security breach, the lobby phone rang. I sprinted to the booth and picked up.

"Hello, Alex?"

"May I speak to the nekkid detective, or is she too busy sunbathing in the buff?"

"That was quick," I said, ignoring the crack. "What'd you find out?"

"The car is registered to the Acme Toy Company. Does that ring any bells?"

CHAPTER 15

ick and I planned our descent into the valley of textiles. After Caltech, the Acme Toy Company was next, then, a final stop at the *Times*. I had to brief Peggy Marshall on our latest developments.

I opened my dresser drawer and out came my old friends panty girdle, Permalift, and nylons. After girding my loins in sweet feminine torture, I stepped into a slip, then donned a smart, no nonsense dress. Today Dick and I were aspiring toyshop owners on the hunt for a supplier.

Again Gatekeeper waved us through as we drove out the gate. I was spending far too much time away from the fun and sun of my nudist hideaway, but I was, after all, working a case. My dream vacation had become a sometime thing.

As the Colorado Street Bridge loomed ahead of us, we discussed our strategy for Acme Toy. Dick said he knew of a speed press on East del Mar that printed business cards while you wait. We stopped there first to order a box of cards for our imaginary shop. We called it Toys and More Toys — "For the Kid Who Has Everything."

With our box of bogus business cards in tow, Dick drove us to Caltech, where his former Stanford school chum, Dr. Hobart Kleff, taught whatever high IQ eggheads teach at Caltech.

Having graduated from a small town high school myself, I never imagined I'd find myself on the grounds of an institute of higher learning like Caltech. Strolling across the campus, I imagined bespectacled scientists decoding the secrets of the universe inside each stately building.

Dr. Kleff's office was on the second floor of the Gates-Thomas Engineering Building. Kleff had a couple years on Dick, but looked much older. He was balding, with a double chin, and plenty of girth around the middle. He wore wire-frame specs and a white lab coat, frayed at the bottom edge. A cigarette clung to his lower lip.

"Dick, you old devil!" Hobart greeted with a slap on the back. "You didn't tell me you were bringing this beautiful young woman with you. If I'm not asking too much, Dick old chum, why not introduce us?"

"Paloma Liu Tsong," Dick began, "Dr. Hobart Kleff, playboy of Caltech's engineering department."

"Dick' always did have a way with words! How do you do, Paloma?" Hobart crooned as he held my hand far too long. He then turned back to Dick.

"You confuse me, Dick," Hobart needled. "You were far too shy to speak to girls at school. Are you a Dale Carnegie graduate now, or did you take a belt of Old Crow? Whatever it was, it worked! My, my! You did well."

"Before you start drooling down your lab coat, Hobart, would you take a minute to look at these microphones?" Dick snapped. "Tell us what you think. And be careful what you say when you take them out of this box. As far as I know, they're still hot."

Dick handed Kleff the cigar box. Kleff carried it to his desk, where he took off the tape and unwrapped the bugs. He placed them under an illuminated magnifying glass on the end of a spring-actuated arm. Turning them over a few times to study their exterior, he took one of the bugs and began prying at it with a small tool. It popped open. His caterpillar eyebrows arched up, then relaxed. He wrapped up the mics, all this in silence, returning them to the cigar box. Finally, he spoke.

"I'm impressed. Very sophisticated stuff," Kleff said. "Far too sophisticated for a toy company. It's got germanium diodes in a highly miniaturized circuit. And since it has no visible connections, I assume it's a wireless unit. Highly advanced. Bell Laboratories developed transistors after the war, but when the government stepped in, they began serious experimentation. If you ask me, and I believe you have, I'd say they're government issue. Where'd you get them, Dick?"

"Like it says on the unit, Hobart, the Acme Toy Company. We're going there today to find out more about them. The city directory says their office is over on North Central, near the park."

Kleff remarked: "If this is an example of what Acme Toy Company can do, it should have it's own wing here in this building."

Dick took the cigar box from Kleff, who then turned his attentions back to me. I yanked my hand from his clutches after a slobbery smooch. Dick thanked Kleff for his help and we were back in Dick's Pontiac with more questions than answers.

"If Kleff is right about these bugs being government issued," I said, "we could be getting into serious trouble, Dick. We'd better play our cards close to the vest."

Dick agreed. "At least we have the business cards. It might give us a bit more credibility. We can be vague about the toy shop angle."

We followed Los Robles Avenue to East Washington, only a few miles from the Institute. The door to Acme Toy Company was on the right side of a nondescript storefront with blacked out windows. We saw no signage on the building to confirm its identity, but painted on the door in nearly indecipherable letters was: "Acme Toy Co."

The squiggly letters, in all-caps, looked like they had been painted by a clown with a two day old case of the DT's. The door, unlocked, opened onto a stairwell ascending to the second story. We began climbing. A thick scent of damp plaster, mixed with stale air, filled the stairwell. Festive posters of the Acme Toy line lined the walls.

Board games, toy guns, clown dolls, friction cars on racetracks, and electric trains made Acme look like a solid company. One toy, though, was of particular interest: the G-Man Spy Kit. The kit had array of eavesdropping devices, a pair of binoculars, and disguises for any up-and-coming junior G-man.

The vacant reception desk at the top of the stairs had a chrome plated bicycle bell. Dick rang it. That brought out an elderly man in a blue and white checked vest, red bow tie, baggy trousers, and pencil mustache. His face nursed a precarious balance of concern and suspicion. I wondered if this was the clown who painted the downstairs door.

"May I help you?" the old gent queried. I gave him one of our cards and began talking.

"We're about to open a toy shop in San Gabriel," I fibbed. "We're looking for a supplier of imaginative toys for our inventory. May we speak with the manager? Is he in?"

"That would be Brace Moreland, but I'm afraid he's not in today." *Brace Moreland*? Karswell's funeral home manager? I hoped the codger didn't notice the look I gave to Dick.

"That's too bad," I said, recovering my composure. "Since your company is right here in Pasadena, it would be a short drive from San Gabriel to pick up an order. That would save us time, and shipping, too."

"I'm afraid we don't sell our toys in California," the bow tie man droned mechanically. "We export our products to other countries."

"That's a shame," Dick said. "You've got some top notch items. I'm sure they'd find a market here in California. We're especially interested in one of your items in particular — the G-Man Spy Kit. May we see one?"

"Well, I don't see why not," he said. "I have a demonstration kit in the storeroom. Let me find it for you."

At that, the red bow tie disappeared through a door that said STORAGE painted in familiar clown-like lettering. I winked at Dick, then glanced into the main office. Men and women in dark business suits sat at work stations, each with its own telephone. A Teletype, the kind used in police departments, chattered in a far corner. Maybe my imagination was working overtime, but I'd swear half the eyes in that office were staring at us. My detective radar also picked up on discrete bulges under the sport coats of several men in the room.

*The ACME
G-MAN KIT*

I turned to Dick, trying not to move my lips. "I've got a creepy feeling about this place," I whispered, "Don't look now, but everyone is staring at us."

"Kiddo," Dick whispered, "the sooner we get out of here the better."

The old gent returned carrying a small box labeled, "G-Man Spy Kit." He laid it on a desk and opened it. We smiled gratefully and sat down to look it over.

"The G-Man Spy Kit is one of our most popular items," the codger explained, "especially at Christmas. It comes with an automatic pistol — plastic of course — a magnifier, a pair of sunglasses, a false nose, a pack of candy cigarettes, and so much more, as you can see."

He forgot to mention the tiny listening device, like the ones we found in Miss Laura's office. I picked one of them up and studied it closely.

"Does this really work?" I asked in contrived awe.

"To some degree, yes." The man explained. "It's something like a crystal radio. It can only pick up voices in the next room at best. It is, after all, a toy."

"May we buy this kit?" Dick asked.

Changing his facial gears from affable to sad, the man said: "I'm afraid not. This kit is our one and only demo, but as I've said, we have a select clientele. They purchase all the toys we make. At the moment we're not taking new clients. I'm sorry."

"We are too," I said. "I guess we'll have to look outside Pasadena now. Well, thanks anyway."

Back on the street, I felt my tension ease, without all those eyes glued to us. I wondered if they knew what we were up to?

Thinking aloud, Dick said: "What kind of company refuses to sell their wares to willing buyers? It makes no sense."

"There's obviously more to the Acme Toy Company than toys," I said. "And it's connected to Karswell's funeral parlor through Brace Moreland."

"Maybe we should take another shot at those two yeggs who kidnapped Rochelle," Dick mused. "They're in the thick of this. We put them on the canvas once, what about going another round?"

"It's a possibility," I replied, "but the payoff might be limited. Why not search Karswell's funeral parlor after closing? What do you think? That might give us a lot more information without being so high profile about it."

"Maybe you're right, but if this is going to be a late night search, Paloma, don't forget that Gatekeeper hits the sack at 10:30. We'll have to spend the night outside Sunland. But that's not a problem. We can stay at my Haskett Court bungalow. I closed it up for vacation, but we can get by for one night."

CHAPTER 16

ick's bungalow court looked like a cottage-lined lane in an old English village. The homes were finished in natural, unpainted stucco. Heavy, wooden timbers supported porch overhangs. Naturally, Dick knew all about the architect who designed it.

"Oddly enough," he prattled, "it's named after the builder, William Haskett, not Charles Ruhe, its architect. The style is English Cottage Revival, and it was built in 1926. My place is the last bungalow at the end of the walk."

Dick unlocked his solid-looking paneled door and we entered a cozy space, as old-fashioned inside as it was on the outside. Dick added some modern touches, though, like the television/ radio/ phonograph console in his living room. He went to the phonograph and slid a few of those new 33 and a third RPM records on the spindle. Debussy's *Clare de Lune* came on. Not surprisingly, Dick was a fan of classical music.

The sofa beckoned me. I plopped down, laid back, and kicked off my shoes. Dick puttered around the room, straightening up. I got the feeling he didn't entertain much.

You know, Dick," I said, "just because we're not in Sunland doesn't mean we can't still be nudists. What do you think?"

Before he could answer I began removing my clothes, and do I know how to take off my clothes! That was my shtick at Andy Wong's Sky Room. I hiked up my skirt to unhook my nylons from Miss Panty Girdle. I rolled down each stocking, slowly, seductively, pulling each one until it stretched a half-mile off my toes. I stood up, unzipped my skirt and stepped out of that. In less time than it takes a jaybird to get naked, I was a nudist again, feeling like my old self. During my blatantly theatrical strip, Dick stood there, transfixed. Numb.

I stuck out my lower lip and pouted, "What are you staring at? You've never seen a naked woman before? What kind of nudist are you?"

Dick was textile free and sitting next to me on that sofa in less than a minute. Maybe Hobart Kleff was right. Dick was a shy guy, slow to get up to speed, but makes up for it at the finish line. Maybe the nudist lifestyle was his way of overcoming his shyness, who knows?

"We forgot our towels," I said, toying with him.

"You know," he mused thoughtfully, "being a confirmed nudist, I often strip when I get home from work. But this is the first time I've been with a like-minded nudist in my home. It kind of makes the outside world seem, well, more inviting."

"Yes it does," I agreed, "And you never know when you'll run into a fellow nudist. Remember Peggy Marshall the *Times* reporter? Turns out she's a nudist too. She said there's a naked beach north of Malibu on the Pacific Coast Highway. She goes there on weekends. It must feel great to swim in the ocean nude. Want to go sometime?"

"Sure. I know the beach she's talking about."

Things were getting cozy and tactile. We were pressed thigh to thigh on the sofa, like the day in the golf cart on our way to Karswell Falls, but this time Sunland rules didn't apply. Hey, I'm only human! I put my hand behind Dick's neck, pulled him close and kissed him on the mouth.

He wasn't shy at all. Before we knew it we were a volcanic eruption of exploding hormones. It became clear we needed more room than the sofa allowed, so I suggested his bedroom. That's where we stayed until midnight, when it came time to break into Karswell's Chapel of the Chimes funeral home.

I felt so relaxed I nearly canceled our plans. But Dick held firm. He went into the kitchen to make coffee, while I gathered my clothing off the living room floor. I zipped up my skirt, snapped on my bra and hosiery, and felt like a department store mannequin again. Dick came in with the coffee, still nude. It felt odd, being clothed again.

"You've got the flashlights and batteries?" I asked.

"Got 'em. Have you got your breaking and entering tools?"

"Check. It won't take long to pick the locks of a corpse emporium like Karswell's. It isn't a high value target for thieves. It'll be easy pickings."

I sipped hot coffee and watched Dick as he dressed. He put on a dark brown pullover, black pants, and a knit cap for less visibility.

The Pontiac made good time. We arrived in Altadena at half past midnight. Dick parked one block away from the funeral home, in the off-chance someone might recognize his car. From there we went to the rear of Karswell's phony Bavarian wikiup. I was right; the lock was a lead pipe cinch. We were inside in less than two minutes.

The parlor was creepier at night, with caskets and flowers looming in the darkness.

"I expected this place to be spooky," I gasped, "but this exceeds my expectations. Let's split up and get this over with. If you take the garage and hearse, I'll go through the upstairs. I want to find Brace Moreland's office."

"I'm on it." Dick replied.

The second story rooms were for staff only. Each room had a sign that described its use, though it was easy enough what went on without the sign. I found the embalming room, a make-up room, a room full of Bavarian costumes, and finally, Brace Moreland's private office. I unlocked the door with my handy lock pick.

Other than the "Miss Funeral Parlor of 1951" calendar on the wall, nothing seemed unusual. Miss August laid back suggestively on a Brinsley Balfore casket with gold plated handles. Moreland's desk should have been the most rewarding trove of goodies, but I saw nothing unusual in the top drawers. The bottom drawer, however, was locked. I took care of that.

A Government Colt automatic like the one the lederhosen dope used on me in Solvang hid under some papers. I was getting warmer. There was an address book underneath the gun. I fanned through the pages and found some names and numbers of interest, three of them for Acme Toy Company. Moreland circled the number for the LA district office of the FBI. Under "S" I found San Pedro Plastics Laboratories. I jotted them all down on a notepad from his desk and slipped them into my pocket. I locked the drawer and moved on to a filing cabinet. It was locked too.

Once inside, I found the biggest bonanza of them all — a manila file folder contained several FBI memorandums rubber-stamped "Eyes Only." One came from J. Edgar Hoover himself, concerning something called Operation Phoenix. Another discussed the Karswell Omega III, with instructions to remove it from the upholstery shop and replace it with a fake. The plan was to transport the original casket to San Pedro Plastics Laboratories where it would undergo "testing."

My goose bumps had goose bumps after I read these. It was time to get out, and fast. I dashed downstairs to find Dick, who was crawling through the rear of the hearse, scouring for clues.

"We have to leave, Dick — now — right away," I rasped frantically.

"But I'm not finished with the hearse yet."

"Forget the hearse! We're in such hot water I've got blisters. Let's go!"

Dick scooted out the back of the hearse and began dusting himself off.

"This is no time for that, Dick! We've got to move-move-move!"

In the dead silence only a funeral parlor can impart, came a sound — a key in the lock on the back door. Someone was entering the building.

"Back in the hearse!" I yelped. "Lie down and cover us with that blanket!"

We hid under the blanket just in time. Someone had entered the lobby. We barely breathed, but we listened intently.

"So, what's the deal this time?" someone asked. "Are we going back to Precision Tool? That place is bad luck for me."

"Stop whining," a deeper voice snapped. "You're just P.O.'d because that chink bimbo and her muscle bound boyfriend bopped us from behind. The boss said he left detailed instructions for us on his desk, and this time we better not screw up. I'll go upstairs and get 'em."

"I'd love to go another round with those two, especially the chink chick. I owe her one for that thing she did to my chest. I ached for days after she did that."

"Don't fret about those two," the deep voice chortled. "Their shelf life is, uh, limited."

A manila file folder contained the big bonanza.

We heard footsteps climb the second story stairs, heading down the hall to Brace Moreland's office. A few minutes passed before the footsteps padded back down the stairs into the lobby.

Deep Voice read Moreland's orders to High Voice: "It says here we're to find a notebook that belonged to Karswell's granddad, something to do with that coffin. Moreland says it's somewhere in the warehouse, and the big brass wants them."

"What's so damn special about that coffin anyway?" High Voice demanded. "All I know is it's the heaviest coffin I ever lifted."

"That's because you aren't observant," Deep Voice chided." You don't listen, so you don't pick up on things. It's some kind of machine, something that a certain colonel wants for the DOD. I hear they've been running tests on it at the San Pedro lab."

High Voice replied: "Whatever. It sounds airy-fairy if you ask me, which you never do. Let's powder. I've had it up to here with this creepy

They've been running tests on it at the San Pedro lab!

joint, and we've got a long haul up the mountain if we want to get to the warehouse tonight."

We exhaled when the door closed behind them.

Climbing out of the hearse I said: "Those guys are G-men, Dick, and not the kind you see in the movies. These are J. Edgar's boys. They'll rob, steal, even kill for him."

We waited another five minutes to make sure they weren't coming back, then rushed back to Dick's car in a brisk walk. If the feds were behind the bugs in Sunland Lodge, and even had us targeted for a possible hit, we were in more trouble than a bear with its nose in a beehive.

Safely back in Dick's ersatz English cottage, we were too upset to sleep. This was one time I didn't want to get naked. My textiles, once too confining for me, suddenly felt safe and cozy. Around four AM we dozed off, fully clothed.

CHAPTER 17

harlie Chan's African Gray parrot stepped off Chan's forearm onto a perch in front of a gathering crowd in the heart of LA's Chinatown. Chan, who billed himself as the "Master of Illusion," had been performing magic here for years.

His act was typical of traditional Chinese magicians, but Chan performed it with such flair, he never failed to draw an audience that wasn't willing to fill his tip jar. His parrot, Li Po, accepted cash gratuities from the crowd by taking the coins in her beak and dropping them into the tip jar on Chan's makeshift stage. This delighted the audience, which encouraged even more tips.

Today Chan had an after-show appointment with crime reporter Peggy Marshall, who was fishing for leads in the Crystal Ball Killer case. She had covered three fortuneteller murders so far, and they all had one thing in common: Chan knew each of the victims. She was connecting dots, looking for a motive in the killings, which still remained elusive, even for the LAPD.

Marshall joined the crowd during the final ten minutes of Chan's act, which always ended in a noxious puff of red smoke from his magic bowl. He bowed, the parrot hopped back onto his arm, and the crowd dispersed. His hand was in the tip jar, counting the crowd's remunerative encouragement, when Marshall introduced herself.

"Mr. Chan? I'm Peggy, from the *Times?*"

"Ah yes, reporter of crime news. Welcome! Please, step into my shop. We can speak freely there."

The Lucky You Gift Shop was a modest Chinatown landmark. Chan sold incense, Lunar New Year gifts, and Chinatown souvenirs to tourists. The magic act was Chan's version of an advertising campaign, a way to promote his shop.

He offered Peggy Marshall a chair with a red silk cushion. He sat opposite Marshall, handing Li Po a handful of pumpkin seeds, which the bird began to shell with her beak.

"Now, what may Chan do for esteemed crime reporter?"

"Mr. Chan, I take it you've read my stories about the three murdered fortunetellers?"

"Yes, very sad. Old friends of mine. Chan think he may be next in line."

"Do you have any idea why someone would want them dead?"

"No. We were friends, yes, but was that reason enough to die?"

"That's what I'm trying to find out. How did you meet them?"

"Interesting tale," Chan replied, lighting several joss sticks in a bowl filled with sand. "Many years ago, there was The Inner Circle."

Marshall's heart leaped. "The Inner Circle? What's that?"

"That was a group of thirteen psychics. Every month, when moon was full, we sit at the big, round table to make contact with other worlds."

"A séance? What year was this?"

"Oh, some 20 years past, 1931 maybe."

"You say there were thirteen? I'm just guessing, but were your three deceased friends part of this group?"

Charlie Chan, Master of Illusion

"You guess correctly, Miss Marshall."

"I would be ever so grateful if you'd write down every member's name, if you can remember them."

"Like it was yesterday, Miss. Chan still got what it takes."

"Oh, I didn't mean..."

"Just kidding. Any further question?"

"Just one: did you have any success contacting these other worlds you spoke of?"

"Oh, yes! We were given blueprint for wonderful machine by great and formidable space being, Ashtar. Ashtar spoke to us from galaxy many light years away."

"What kind of machine was it?"

"It alter time," Chan explained. "Go back, go forward, like magic."

"You mean it was some sort of time machine?"

"Chan suppose you might call it that, yes."

"I know I said that would be my last question, but please tell me, who presided over your group? Did it have a leader?"

"Yes, Cranston Karswell, a most brilliant inventor. He reside with ancestors now."

"Karswell? Any relation to Jerome Karswell, the Hollywood psychic?"

"His honorable grandfather."

Chan wrote the names of Karswell's group on the back of an ad for Chinese herbs. While Chan was writing, Marshall perused the shop and purchased a silk blouse as a gesture of thanks. Chan had just given her the break she had been looking for, and the Karswell connection overlapped her case with mine. As soon as she returned to the office she called Sunland Lodge. Miss Laura informed her I was in Pasadena, but expected me back any time.

I was still in Dick's bungalow, feeling guilty that I dragged him into a case that turned out to be far more than a missing coffin caper. Over hot coffee in the cozy breakfast nook of his cottage kitchen, I tried to back him off the case.

"Forget everything that happened in Altadena last night, Dick," I warned. "Go back to Sunland and enjoy your vacation and you'll get no more trouble from me. I'll talk to my partner about these latest developments. I'll fill in Peggy Marshall too. Maybe my only protection is the free press."

"I'm afraid it's too late to back out now, Paloma. If the feds have been listening in to what went on in Miss Laura's office, they know plenty by now: like our names, our relatives, friends, and who knows what else?"

"I know, I know. I'm sorry I got you into this mess, Dick."

"It's a mess for sure, but nudists don't back down, and they don't take crap from the Man. Besides, you can't take on the feds single handed."

We decided to leave LA and return to the illusion of safety we felt at Sunland. Dick closed up the bungalow and we drove to the nearest drugstore, where I found a phone booth, shut the door, and dialed Alex. Having nothing better to do, he picked up right away.

"Alex, is Nurse Ilsa within earshot?" I asked.

"Nope, she just left, what's up?"

"Plenty. The feds are involved in our case. We're being watched."

"We who?"

"Me, Dick Barnett our camp counselor, Laura Borealis, our camp administrator, and more likely than not, Peggy Marshall, the crime reporter at the *Los Angeles Times*. The feds bugged the Sunland Lodge. They're keeping tabs on everyone. Alex, we're in hot water."

"I'm calling from a drugstore phone booth. I won't be making any more calls from private phones. Do you still have your contact with the FBI up there?"

"It's been awhile since we talked, but we're still on good terms, why?"

"Do you think he'd be willing to talk about something called Project Phoenix? I saw that name on a top secret FBI memorandum. It's very important to my case."

"You're reading top secret FBI communiqués now?" Alex screeched over the wire. "No wonder you're in trouble! Okay, okay, I'll call my contact, but I can't guarantee he'll drop a dime on J. Edgar. Depends on his mood. Maybe he's tired of hounding Charlie Chaplin and I'll brighten his day."

"Thanks, I need all the help I can get. I'm in way over my head on this. It appears Karswell's missing coffin is part of a government cover-up."

"Okay, Kitten, I'll get back to you. This'll give me something to do between sponge baths. *Ciao*."

I hung up the receiver and then dialed Peggy Marshall's desk at the *Times*. She picked up right away.

"Marshall talking."

"Peggy? Paloma. Our case has amped up a notch. I want to fill you in on what we've learned, in case something happens to me."

"It's that serious? Wait! I have important news to tell you."

"Before you do, call me from a pay phone there, okay? Here's my number."

I waited in the booth five minutes while Peggy went to the public phone in her office. My phone rang and I picked up right away.

"It turns out you were right, Paloma. We're working on the same case. I now have a probable motive for the Crystal Ball Killer, and the tie-in is your Incredible Karswell's grandfather."

"Peggy, nothing surprises me about this case," I shivered. "The feds have Karswell's funeral home staked out, and they've bugged the office at Sunland Lodge. It looks like Karswell's manager Brace Moreland is tied up in this somehow. He's turned up at the Acme Toy Company, a front for something called Project Phoenix. Maybe it's a call center or something, because they sure aren't selling toys. And you're right. Whatever this is, it's connected to grandfather Karswell's coffin. This is big, Peggy!"

"That's putting it mildly," Marshall replied. "I've just come from Chinatown. That's where I got my lead on a motive in the Crystal Ball Killer case. But with so many ears pressed to the wall on this, let's talk in person. Do you know Hancock Park, where the La Brea Tar Pits are on Wilshire?"

"I can find it."

"Okay, meet me there at nine tonight. By that time the tourists have gone and the place is empty. We can talk there without being heard or disturbed. I'll wait for you next to the statue of the mastodon in the tar pit."

"Swell, see you there at nine," I said, and rung off.

The Inner Circle

CHAPTER 18

t took a lot of convincing, but I assured Dick it would be perfectly safe for me to meet Peggy Marshall at Hancock Park that night.

"You know that I can take care of myself, Dick." I said. I wonder what was I thinking? He even let me borrow the Pontiac.

Traffic was light, and I found plenty of parking on Wilshire. My Phillips 66 street map of Los Angeles said I was directly in front of Hancock Park. Having never been to the La Brea Tar Pits before, I didn't know what to expect.

Maybe the LA Chamber of Commerce knew more than I did, but why the city of Los Angeles kept a noxious pit of bubbling crude oil in the middle of a public park was beyond me. I'd been told that tourists flock here by the dozens, posing for snapshots in front of the bubbling, black goo.

Naturally, Dick knew all about the tar pits. Besides being full of the skeletons of prehistoric beasts, the LAPD has been known to drag them for bodies of missing persons. Only one turned up so far, and she had been lying in the goop for 9,000 years.

Peggy was right; the park was deserted — and dark. Car headlights zooming along Wilshire Blvd. looked miles away. I positioned myself near the concrete statue of what looked like a prehistoric elephant; the mastodon Peggy mentioned. It was hard to imagine that elephants used to live where downtown LA is now.

An evening breeze brought welcome relief from the summer heat. The sun had warmed up the tar pit all day, and a pungent aroma of raw crude hung over the black lake in a sulfurous cloud. Peggy was already fifteen minutes late, and I'd rather be anywhere but here.

I was getting anxious, and checked my wristwatch every few minutes. Peggy was now 30 minutes late. Dark thoughts snaked their way into my gray matter. Something must have happened to her. Maybe her car crashed. Maybe she was kidnapped. I was about to abandon my post to hunt for a phone booth when I noticed a silhouette coming my way. At last, Peggy had arrived. But as she got closer, I knew I was mistaken.

This wasn't Peggy, it was one of the lederhosen twins. He held a howitzer in his mitt and was closing in. I had nowhere to go.

"Put 'em up, NOW!" the creep ordered.

What else could I do? I think he remembered our last two encounters, because he kept his distance. I couldn't get close enough to smack him.

"Turn around and face the street!" he snarled.

My options were sparse; zero, in fact. I stood there, staring at the traffic on Wilshire, waiting for the blast from his automatic. Instead, I felt his foot against the small of my back. He pushed me. Hard! Before I could swing around to slug him, I stumbled into the pit.

He watched me as the tar took hold, then backed off and disappeared in the darkness. I was about to find out what that mastodon over there discovered when it wandered into his pit of prehistoric flypaper.

I'd never fallen into a tar pit before, which, as Dick informed me earlier, was not tar at all. It was a type of asphalt made of thick oil.

The La Brea Tar Pit

Unlike the mastodon, I knew all about the tenacious killer I faced. It bubbled up from the Salt Lake Oil Field, seeping through the Sixth Street Fault. And it held on to me tighter than a used car salesman.

I didn't sink as far or as fast as I thought I would. Not yet anyway, so I tried not to struggle. If I lost my balance and fell, it was curtains for sure, and no one would ever know what happened to me. I would simply disappear.

What irony! In the heart of the biggest city in California, I was sinking into a prehistoric death trap for saber-tooth tigers. I tried calling for help, but the pit muffled my cries. The traffic on Wilshire kept moving along as though all was right with the world. I was too far away for anyone to hear.

This was a private eye's lot in life, I thought; snuffed out in the line of duty. My only consolation was that some day, my death would appear in Ripley's Believe or Not.

The goo reached my thighs as I continued to sink. My shoes must have come off when I stumbled into the pit, because I felt it oozing between my toes.

Remind me to mail a complaint to the Los Angeles Chamber of Commerce. A tourist attraction like this was far too dangerous for a public park. I thought about my complaint letter as long as I could, to keep my mind off my dwindling lifespan. Worst of all, I'd never get this tar out of my new dress. I'd include my dry-cleaning bill with the complaint letter, I mused.

From somewhere beyond my thoughts, a voice broke through: "Paloma! Over here! Grab hold of this!"

I was hearing voices now. That was not unusual in situations like this. One's life flashes before one's eyes, and maybe voices pop out of nowhere. Things like that have been known to happen. The voice did sound familiar, though. I scanned the shore where a dark figure held out a metal pole in my direction. It sounded like Dick's voice, but that couldn't be. I left him at the cottage without his car.

Trying not to fall, I stretched as far as I could to reach the end of the pole, grabbed the end and held on with a vengeance. The dark figure began pulling, but the pit wouldn't let go. It held on tight to my legs, my dress, everything. I was tipping over.

"Careful!" the voice yelped. "Stay upright! Pull up one leg at a time and try to walk while I pull."

I didn't ask if it was really Dick, or why Peggy Marshall never showed up. All I wanted was to be out of that pit. I moved my legs a few inches at a time, but whenever I put my foot back down, I began sinking again. With so much resistance from the pit, I was losing strength. Then I felt something solid underneath, sloping up toward shore. I moved more forcefully with solid ground underfoot. Five minutes later I was back on solid ground. For a while, I just sat, exhausted.

"Are you really Dick Barnett?" I moaned. His words whirled around me like a tornado.

"Who did you think it was? I got a call from Peggy after you'd left," he blathered. "She said she wanted to reschedule your meeting after you'd cancelled it. I told her you hadn't canceled it, that you were on your way to the tar pits. It sounded like a set-up. So, I called a taxi and came right over. Boy, do you smell bad, and no wonder! Did you know that pit is full of methane gas?"

"I'll write that down later, Dick, but now I feel terrible! I want out of these clothes! I'll never see my favorite pumps again. They're somewhere in — THERE." I said, pointing a gooey finger at the pit.

"C'mon, kiddo, I think you're in a state of shock. There's a blanket in the car. Good thing I brought my extra set of car keys. We'll wrap you up and take you back to the bungalow. I'm not sure how we'll get this asphalt off, though."

"Step out of the dress," he said.

Dick may have been right about the shock. All I could think of was an ice cream sundae. I told Dick I wanted one, NOW. He said I couldn't go to an ice cream shop covered in crude.

As I stood shivering next to his Pontiac, he wrapped me in a wool blanket. Next thing I knew, we were back in his bungalow. He spread a canvas tarp on the kitchen floor as I watched. He took my arm, guiding me to the center of the tarp, then stripped down to his boxer shorts.

Wiping off the goo, he found the zipper on the back of my dress. The zipper jammed, so he rubbed a bar of soap on it and it began to move again. My dress fell with a thud onto the tarp.

"Okay, Paloma," he ordered. "Step out. First your right leg, then the left." His voice echoed from a canyon far, far away, but I obeyed and stepped out of the dress. That exposed my oil-soaked feminine foundations. Those were more complicated and took more time to remove. Dick had to wipe tar from my garters before he could unsnap them, and from the way he struggled, I could tell he'd never unfastened a woman's nylons before. He unhooked my Permalift bra, removing it from my mounded marvels. Thankfully, they were tarless, and grateful to hang free.

He began wiping me from the waist down, using hand towels as rags, and when my skin began to redden, he marched me into the shower with a bar of soap.

"Start scrubbing," he said, shoving a dozen washcloths into my limp hands. "See how much you can clean off with soap and hot water. Take your time."

After abrading myself raw for half an hour, I gave up. I still smelled like a freshly paved highway, but so what? After I find the dope that did this to me, I won't care what I smell like. I was ready to bring down his entire shady operation.

CHAPTER 19

irst thing next morning, Dick drove me to a Rexall drugstore on Colorado Blvd. where I slipped into a phone booth and dialed the public phone at the *Times*. No more private phones for me, and that included Peggy Marshall's. By now the feds had her line tapped, too.

Peggy was waiting near her appointed phone booth for my call and picked up on the first ring. Relieved to hear I was okay, she said she got worried about me last night after talking to Dick. This time, she agreed to meet me at the drugstore right away.

The store had an ice cream counter with a soda jerk on duty. One of the house specialties was a Route 66 ice cream sundae. Colorado Blvd. and Route 66 were the same highway, get it? I couldn't imagine what a Route 66 sundae would taste like, so I ordered one. Its selling point was small slab of chocolate in the shape of a Route 66 highway sign. It stuck out of two scoops of ice cream. I ate the whole thing while I waited for Peggy and ordered another.

Once Peggy arrived, we moved to the far end of the counter where we could talk in private. I gave her the gory details of my near death experience in the tar pits, and she gave me the lowdown on Karswell's granddad.

"We've been working on the same case all along, Paloma," Marshall said. "We just didn't realize it until the clues began to overlap. I tracked down this Chinese magician who knew all three victims, a local named Charlie Chan. When he told me that he, and the murder victims all belonged to a group of psychics called The Inner Circle, things began to jell.

"And here's where our cases collide, Paloma," Marshall continued with bated breath. "The leader of the group was *Cranston* Karswel, Jerome Karswell's grandfather."

I said: "So each one of the Crystal Ball Killer's victims belonged to the group?"

"That's right! I've looked up every name on a member list Chan gave to me. There are only three members still alive, Chan being one of them."

I swallowed another helping of ice cream. "Did he say anything about the Omega III, Karswell's missing coffin. That's what brought me into the case, when the Incredible Karswell's wife hired me to find that coffin.

"This is strictly off the record, Peggy, but Dick and I broke into Karswell's Altadena funeral parlor. I saw top-secret FBI memorandums in Brace Moreland's office that confirmed the feds stole the Omega III and took it to a lab in San Pedro. They're doing some kind of experiments with it. Seems it's more than just a coffin with martini amenities as Jerome thought. It's some kind of machine."

"Yes that's right!" Peggy blurted with enough exclamation to make the soda jerk look our way. Peggy noticed, and quieted down.

"That's the important part," she whispered. "According to Chan, that coffin can alter time. He was there when Karswell channeled the blueprints for it. He said the plans came from some sort of alien being. It all sounds too crazy for words, but why would the feds throw so much personnel and money at a coffin?

"That makes three of those you've eaten since I've been here."

"Anyway, to sum it all up, Paloma, what we've got is a machine from outer space and a serial killer knocking off anyone that knows about it. I'd sure like to find that San Pedro lab."

Our conversation ended when the soda jerk returned.

He smiled. "Can I bring you ladies anything else?"

"I'll take another ice cream sundae," I replied. "This time, more nuts, two of those little road signs, and a double scoop of whipped cream. Oh, and an extra cherry."

He raised his eyebrows. "You got it, Miss."

Peggy whistled. "So far, that makes three sundaes, Paloma. How do you stay so slim?"

"At the rate I'm going, I won't be much longer. It was that hellish tar pit. It gave me an awful craving for ice cream sundaes. Breathing those noxious fumes in that oily crud made me crave something sweet, cold, and creamy. But, you said you'd like to know where that lab is? Guess what? I wrote down the phone number from Brace Moreland's address book. Why not call the operator and get the address that goes with the number?"

"Paloma, you're amazing!" Peggy yelped.

The soda jerk returned and put down a fresh Route 66 sundae next to my two empties. We waited for him to return to the other end of the counter before resuming our exchange.

"Here's the thing, Peggy," I said as low as possible. "If those fortunetellers were killed for what they knew about the Omega III, one could assume Project Phoenix is the glue that holds this entire plot together."

"I think you're right," Peggy nodded. "We have to be extremely cautious. You've already been attacked twice and survived. But now we know the Omega III's true purpose. If we're ever found out, we'll find our names on the Crystal Ball Killer's hit list too. Even walking across the street could be dangerous if we let down our guard. Stick close to other people, and keep your eyes peeled for anything that seems unusual, even at Sunland. I've got to get back to the office and tie up all these loose ends with a great big bow before I turn in my story. This could be the high point of my newspaper career."

I finished my last sundae as we wrapped up our meeting. Peggy left first, and I walked out a few minutes later. Dick waited patiently in the Pontiac. I opened the passenger door and slid onto the front seat. Dick had lowered the convertible top and the Naugahyde upholstery had been baking in the sun. Luckily, I wasn't naked; my rear would have been scalded. For some reason, Dick looked pleased with himself.

"While you two traded notes," he explained, I went shopping at San Miguel's Gun and Ammo Shop across the street. Take a look at this!"

He pulled out a blue finished snub nose .32 revolver.

"It fits perfectly into my hip pocket."

This meant Dick was getting nervous, too.

"Just don't keep it in the glove compartment" I said. "In every detective movie I've ever seen, the killer takes it out of the glove compartment, shoots somebody, then leaves it at the scene of the crime."

"Don't you worry about that. I'm keeping this baby where I can get it in a hurry."

I gave him a skeptical glance.

"What?" Dick groused.

"That's an interesting plan," I said. "for a nudist. I'm curious where you'll keep it on you at Sunland."

"Oh. Right. It'll be pretty obvious at camp, won't it. How about this? I'll keep it in a pack slung over my shoulder."

"Swell," I said. "Just keep the safety on."

Driving back to Sunland, I thought every car that came too close was full of G-men ready to shoot us or push us off the road. I asked Dick to pull over in Altadena to find another phone booth. I had to call Alex.

Maybe he learned something from his FBI informant. He had, and he sounded worried.

"The good news is, my informant turned whistle blower," Alex began. "The bad news is you're too hot to handle, Moon Cakes. That thing you mentioned called Project Phoenix? That's what made my stoolie turn on J. Edgar. He still has a few scruples, I guess. Project Phoenix is a top-secret operation about a machine that can warp time. Look, I'm just telling you what he told me. Anyone who believes this junk must be..."

"Okay, okay, Alex!" I squawked. "I know it sounds crazy! What else did he say?"

"My, my, we are testy today! Well, my contact also mentioned a research lab where government scientists are experimenting with this thing, whatever it is. They used it to bring back a serial killer from the future to do the feds' dirty work. I swear, they must read *Amazing Stories* to come up baloney like this. He claims they did it this way because the killer doesn't exist in our time, and has to record. Kooky, huh?"

"Yeah, kooky. What else?"

"They brought this time traveling Jack the Ripper from up here. A place called Vallejo. He was, I mean he will be very bad news somewhere in the future, but now that he's here, he's bad news here. The feds got the guy to start bumping off anyone who knew anything about that machine. I mean, if this were all true, I wouldn't want to know anything about it. But thanks to you, I do!"

"Yeah, yeah, I know, Alex. If my shadow touches you, you'll die."

"How much did you say you were getting paid for this train wreck? Whatever it is, it's not enough. You'll spend more than that on funeral arrangements. Oops, gotta go. Nurse Ilsa just brought in my pipe and slippers. *Ciao.* Oh, and good luck, Angel. Don't call me, I'll call you."

"Thanks for the encouragement, Alex."

I slammed down the receiver and dashed out of the drugstore to the Pontiac.

"Let's get out of here, Dick!"

Without asking what or why, Dick stomped the gas pedal so hard I got pressed into the seat. The Pontiac took off at top speed. I let out a sigh of relief when I saw the city limits sign zip by. Miracle of miracles, we reached the mountain road in one piece and were at the front gate waiting for Gatekeeper, honking to bring him down. Twenty minutes later, we were heading up the dirt road to our cabins.

Frolicking naked in the woods didn't feel so free anymore. The feds had ruined my vacation. On top of that, the La Brea Tar Pits incident was still simmering in the cauldron of my darkest thoughts. I craved to return the favor.

CHAPTER 20

 vy Wyldwind didn't know it, but she was one of only three Inner Circle members left alive. She had been out of touch with her teammates for years, running into them only by chance at a local psychic fair. Last year she met several members at Cranston Karswell's funeral.

Like most Angelinos, Wyldwind read the *Times*. She knew about the cold-blooded killer stalking her fellow psychics, all members of Karswell's Inner Circle. That made her skittish. Was it merely a coincidence? Why would someone target her former associates from a time she barely remembered? It had to be coincidence, she thought. They were simply in the wrong place at the wrong time. That made her less cautious than she should have been.

She lived on 4th Street at the top of the Bunker Hill Library steps in a weathered Victorian fourplex, once home to a 19th Century banker and his family. The 20th Century marked a significant shift in the population of Bunker Hill. Working-class families began replacing well-to-do Angelino homeowners after the First World War. The banker finally sold the family home and moved to Westwood, and, like many Bunker Hill mansions, the banker's stately home became four apartments and was rented out. As low rent housing, its paint blistered and its gingerbread trim fell off and was never replaced.

This was where Ivy Wyldwind divined the fortunes of bored housewives, shop clerks, shoe salesmen — anyone willing to pay her to tell them how their lives would change for the better. Tonight Ivy Wyldwind would learn the identity of the Crystal Ball Killer, maybe even the name of his next victim. The moon was full, and she'd had her evening glass of sherry. If successful, she would inform the police and foil the killer's plans. She downed a second glass of sherry and put out Madame Blavatsky, her Siamese cat, so as not to be disturbed. Madame Blavatsky had a knack for interfering with Wyldwind 's link to the Unknown.

Her crystal ball was made of quartz. Before it was a crystal ball it had been a six-foot Brazilian crystal, mined from a cavern in the Amazon

Ivy Wyldwind would discover the identity of the Crystal Ball Killer

rainforest. She placed it on its mahogany stand and lulled herself into a deep trance.

Staring into the crystal, she saw busy downtown streets, Union Station, and Chinatown in quick succession. She poured a third glass of sherry. Maybe that's what did it. A dark shape appeared inside her crystal sphere, hard to make out, but slowly coming into focus as a hooded figure in black robes; an ominous figure, and familiar. She had seen a sketch of the same figure on wanted posters all over town. A prickly sensation played on the back of her neck. That was when she knew the image was not confined to her crystal ball. It was the reflection of someone standing behind her. She was about to meet the Crystal Ball Killer in the flesh!

Frozen in fear, her eyes followed the figure in the glass as it reached for her. Its thick fingers found her throat and began squeezing. She struggled. Caught in the killer's vice-like grip, the lack of oxygen made her light-headed. The pain of her crushed windpipe was excruciating. But it didn't last long. She was dead within minutes. When the killer knew she had stopped breathing, he dropped her lifeless body to the floor.

A hammer appeared from under his robe. He raised it high above Ivy Wyldwind's crystal ball, and it came down in one powerful blow, shattering the crystal. Gently now, he placed an envelope addressed to Peggy Marshall on the table. His job here was done.

The killer's robes made a muffled, rustling sound as he left the room. Madame Blavatsky, Wyldwind's Siamese cat, ran inside as he opened the back door.

An anonymous phone call sent police to the murder scene. After reading the killer's note, they gave it to Peggy Marshall, who reprinted it in her *Times* story with the headline: *Fortuneteller Killer Strikes Again!* It read: "I am the one who killed the three other fortunetellers. This makes four. The LAPD cannot stop me. Print this letter on the front page of the *Times* or I shall kill again!"

He would kill again regardless of what Peggy Marshall did or did not do.

CHAPTER 21

Safely inside Dick's Owl Cottage, we planned our next move. Sticking to camp rules, we stripped — though not as eagerly as we used to. Our carefree vacation was over. We had been swept up in a deadly game of cat and mouse, and we were the mice. A dark cloud had settled over Dick. His mood had become decidedly downbeat.

"Even if the killer doesn't track us down and kill us," he surmised, "we've still got the feds on our backs. Who knows what they've got planned."

"We still have Peggy Marshall, Dick!" I said with the best Pollyanna smile I could muster. "She's working on her expose and has connections inside the LAPD. She'll expose Operation Phoenix and that'll be the end of them."

My pep talk was pathetic and I knew it. Dick wasn't convinced. We had to fend for ourselves, he said.

"Peggy's not a sure thing, not at all, Paloma. We can't count on anyone but us. We have to stick together, keep an eye on each other. From now on you'd better start sleeping here in my cabin. I've got a double bed with a .32 under the pillow. I'd worry less if I knew your whereabouts after lights out."

I had to admit, Dick's plan had appeal. After all, I'm only human. He proved that last night in his bungalow.

"Good thinking, Dick," I trilled, trying to reign in my vocal cords. "I'll need a few things from next door. Be right back."

I thought about walking to the lodge to speak with Laura Borealis, but it was getting late and I was tired. We'd talk tomorrow. The Karswells were clueless about the true nature of the Karswell coffin, so they were safe. And I sure wasn't going to tell them about it, at least, not yet.

Jaybird Cottage looked exactly as I'd left it. I tossed a few items into a canvas tote and 15 minutes later was back inside Owl Cottage. Five minutes after that the Lights Out bell chimed. Dick snapped off the cabin lights and lit a candle in the living room.

"I'm going to take a shower before bed," he announced. "I won't be long."

As Dick showered, I sat in the dark listening to the sound of running water.

Maybe it was my imagination, but I could swear I still felt oily from that tar pit. Then I got lonely and decided there was enough room in Dick's shower for us both, so I joined him.

Dick scrubbed my back. He told me it looked clear and I didn't smell like oil. When he'd finished I turned around and pressed my feminine hardware into his chest. Like I said, I'm only human. The hot, soapy water combined with Dick's muscles calmed my jitters. It also put a quick end to our shower. We toweled off and slipped into bed, trying our best to forget the last 48 hours. Much to my satisfaction, Dick couldn't have tried much harder.

• • •

The morning sun rose over the San Gabriel Mountains as I slipped out of bed and tiptoed into the next room while Dick slept. I wanted to listen to the morning news broadcast. When the tubes warmed up on Dick's RCA Victor radio, the outside world came pouring in.

The Crystal Ball Killer had struck again. A fortuneteller named Ivy Wyldwind had been added to his list. Although the newscaster didn't say so, I'd bet my Permalift that Ivy Wyldwind belonged to the ill-fated Inner Circle. The killer used the same props, too: a cryptic note taunting the LAPD was found next to Wyldwind's smashed crystal ball. Part of the note was in code.

The killer claimed his identity was hidden in the code, if the cops could figure it out. The LAPD's cryptology team had been working day and night on codes found at each murder scene, with no luck.

I had to get down to the lodge and pick up a *Times* newspaper before the other guests snapped them up first. I knew Peggy Marshall would have covered this murder in more detail, or, as much as the cops wanted her to know about it.

As gently as I could, I cooed: "Dick, wake up." All was quiet.

Never mind. I slipped out the door and ankled down to the lodge, where I found one last copy of the *Times* on the front desk. I rolled up the paper and sprinted back to Owl Cottage, where I found Dick's face still plastered to his pillow. With the open palm of my hand I gave his chiseled hindquarters a swift smack.

"Hey! If you want breakfast you'd better get a move on, big guy!"

Dick must have been exhausted to nearly sleep through his breakfast. Since there was no need to get dressed, we were seated at the Mess Hall's long, U-shaped table in no time. Freckle-faced Rochelle was serving meals, working her way down our side of the table. She wore fewer band-aids today, but no less freckles.

"So? Where have you two been hiding?" she pried. "I was beginning to think you'd eloped or something."

"Ha ha, Rochelle," I grouched. "We were hoping to get some rest now that we're back, if you get my drift."

Nodding her head, she gave me a sly wink. "'Nuff said, Paloma. Anyone for coffee?"

Dick raised his hand. "I'll take some," he mumbled, eyelids half closed.

Rochelle fastened Dick with a beady eyed stare. Clearly, her imagination was running wild. She filled his cup from a Pyrexcarafe. Dick picked it up, blowing on the hot coffee before taking a sip. But Rochelle continued to hover over him.

"It must have been real important," she prodded. "To leave camp, I mean."

"Wha?" Dick rasped. "Oh, yes, very. We had to attend a funeral."

Rochelle fastened a knowing look on me with her pale blue sparklers.

"Yeah, right. Anyone for hotcakes and vegan breakfast sausage?"

CHAPTER 22

eggy Marshall used the phone number from Brace Moreland's address book to pinpoint the San Pedro laboratory. She'd called Sunland Lodge from a pay phone at the *Times* to leave a message with Miss Laura. She and Lt. Frank Dangelo of the LAPD were heading to San Pedro to take a look at San Pedro Plastics Laboratory, she said.

Dangelo was skeptical of Peggy's claims, especially the one about the killer's link to a secret cabal of federal agents embedded in Los Angeles. Nevertheless, Peggy's reputation as a crime reporter was enough for him to follow up on her lead. He requisitioned an unmarked Ford sedan and a uniformed officer as his driver and backup. Dangelo chewed over Peggy Marshall's findings on their way to the site.

"To me, all this stuff about a coffin and a secret government plot sounds like an episode from *The Phantom Creeps*," Dangelo grunted, gnawing on the end of his stogie. "If you hadn't given me the dope on that Hargrove murder case last year, I wouldn't be here now."

"Humor me, Lieutenant," Marshall replied. "It all sounded crazy to me, too — at first — but there's already been two attempts on a private investigator's life by federal agents, and three murders connected to this case. On top of that, there was the kidnapping of a Los Angeles citizen by the same agents. The feds have put a lot of manpower into this operation, and they'll do whatever it takes to keep it secret, even if that means using a professional assassin."

They found San Pedro Plastics Laboratories in a warehouse district near the San Pedro waterfront on West Beacon Street. A sign out front said the building belonged to the Benevolent Sisters of the Poor. Dangelo got out of his cruiser to look for a window. There were none. He sent his officer around back to look there. Five minutes later, the cop reappeared.

"Lieutenant! There's a fire escape going up to the roof. There's gotta be a skylight up there. We might try that."

"Lead the way, O'Shaughnessy."

It was an easy climb on a one-story building, which had three skylights up top. Treading lightly, they found a skylight and looked down. They saw plenty. The lab was straight out of a Flash Gordon epic, full of weird electronic gizmos. Bolts of blue lightning zapped between two massive Tesla coils. But Peggy's attention focused on a hooded figure in black robes, talking to two men in lab coats.

"Do you see what I see, Lieutenant?"

"You bet I do. That's our man!"

"I wonder what they're talking about?" Peggy wondered aloud.

"Who they'll be killing next, I'll wager," Dangelo replied. "I'm going to call for backup. We can't storm the Bastille with just two cops. There's no telling how many clowns they've got in that circus down there. I'll head back to the car."

Peggy and officer O'Shaughnessy remained topside while Dangelo climbed back down the ladder to his cruiser. He radioed headquarters, told them to bring plenty of back-up, and nix the sirens.

"I want to surprise them," he said.

Within minutes, six black and whites pulled up in front of San Pedro Plastics Laboratory, lights flashing. Cops piled out of each car brandishing their weapons. Dangelo barked out orders.

"Olson! Did you bring the battering ram? Good. You three, cover the front door. Holcomb and Simms, you cover the back. I don't want anyone to get away."

Holding their positions, they waited for Dangelo's signal. He waved his hand in the air and brought it down in a sweeping motion. Three cops picked up the battering ram and

Peggy Marshall watched the hooded figure in black robes.

charged the front door. It took several tries before it gave way, which was time enough for those inside to prepare for action.

As the first wave of officers rushed in, they were met with gunfire. Several cops were pinned down, returning fire nonetheless. Dangelo's main target was the hooded figure who had ducked behind a counter, firing a .45 in his direction. The officer next to Dangelo went down, hit by one of the killer's lead pills.

There were at least a dozen men in the warehouse — all wearing dark suits and thick-soled shoes. One of them had a machine gun, making life miserable for the cops. A second wave of LAPD rushed the door, gats blazing. The tide was turning in favor of the LAPD. Finally, Dangelo yelled:

"Cease fire!"

Shots from the opposing side dwindled. Then, things got quiet. A thick, white smoke filled the warehouse.

Turning on his bullhorn, Dangelo announced: "This is Lieutenant Dangelo of the Los Angeles Police Department. Either throw out your weapons, or I'll call for more backup and we'll blast you from here to kingdom come. Let's see those hands in the air!"

For a while, there was only silence. The feds were weighing their options. At last, one pistol clattered to the floor, then another, until dozens littered the warehouse.

Dangelo rasped, "Where's that tommy gun?"

It, too, hit the floor.

A voice from inside the lab pierced the stifling gun smoke: "You're interfering with a government operation, Lieutenant. We're federal agents. You can check our badges if you don't believe me."

"Yeah?" Dangelo snorted. "Your government operation committed murder on my turf, friend. Until J. Edgar springs you, you're coming with us."

"I guess you've got to learn the hard way, huh, Lieutenant?"

"That may be, but you're still coming with us. Boys, make sure you've got their weapons. Don't leave anyone behind. Where's that hooded S.O.B.? I want him, NOW!"

Several feds, hands clasped behind their heads, walked toward the armed officers, who cuffed and escorted them to the waiting squad cars. The last one out the door confronted Dangelo.

"You'll find my badge inside my coat pocket," the fed growled through clenched grinders. "Go ahead, take a close look."

Dangelo took it out, checked the ID.

"My, my, you're a G-man. Too bad you drilled one of my men. And since you failed to fill us in this operation, we have no idea what you've been up to. You could be a pack of rogue agents for all I know. Maybe J. Edgar will be happy you're behind bars. Get moving."

Dangelo counted heads but found no hooded killer.

"Scour the lab, boys! I don't see the guy in the hood!"

The search revealed a trap door that led to a tunnel beneath the building. Two cops followed it to a stairwell exiting through an empty lot on the next block. The killer was long gone.

"Damn it all to hades!" Dangelo cursed. "Those feds will get sprung before the ink is dry on our booking sheet, and the guy I really wanted, the one standing here as black as sin, took a powder! How did this happen?"

Peggy Marshall replied: "You were right, Lieutenant. This does look like an episode from *The Phantom Creeps*. I suggest we take a ride to the Acme Toy Company. Your man may have gone there."

A second wave of cops rushed in, gats blazing.

CHAPTER 23

The hooded figure took Route 66 across the Colorado Street Bridge into Pasadena. He hung a left on Lake and broke a few traffic laws to reach Altadena, where he stashed his heap behind the Karswell Chapel of the Chimes funeral home. No one saw him slip through the back door.

It had been a slow day at Chapel of the Chimes. Death, it seemed, had taken the day off.

Johann and Herman were in the garage, killing time, unaware of the shootout in San Pedro. The hooded figure crept up the stairs to Brace Moreland's office and disappeared inside.

Johann, sitting on an upturned barrel, chain smoked one cigarette after another.

"When do you think we'll get reassigned out of this dump? I never want to see another coffin again, especially if it's mine."

"It's not our job to wonder, Johann. We get orders and we execute them. That's it."

Silent far too long, the wall phone finally jangled its unpleasant tune and startling Johann. He dropped his cigarette on the floor. His voice went up an octave when he cried:

"Maybe that's him!"

"Yeah, or maybe the blonde broad is calling from the office and wants us to move another casket into the chapel."

"She hasn't come back from lunch yet," Johann replied. "She takes awful long lunches. What do you think she's up to?"

The phone continued ringing.

"Are you going to answer that?"

Johann slid off the barrel and answered the phone.

"Garage."

The voice on the other end of the line made Johann snap to attention. He listened intently.

"Yeah, got it, sir, no problem. We're on top of it. Right away!"

He hung up the phone and turned to Herman, who had only heard one side of the conversation.

"It was Moreland," Johann explained. "The cops raided the San Pedro lab. He wants us to get over there, find the damn coffin and take it to the Precision Tool warehouse. Then we wait there for further instructions. Said we have to be careful. There were boatloads of cops there this morning."

So, we're the clean-up crew," Herman moaned. "Better take our heaters. And forget the lederhosen! I feel like an idiot wearing these short pants in public."

The agents swapped their Oktoberfest duds for one-piece mechanic's jump suits. Johann unlocked the garage's timbered Bavarian double doors while Herman maneuvered the hearse onto the street. They headed for San Pedro.

At that very moment, Peggy Marshall, Lieutenant Dangelo, and officer O'Shaughnessy were dropping anchor in front of the Acme Toy Company.

The hooded figure took Route 66 to Pasadena.

"This is it," Marshall said. "The control center is upstairs."

The police cruiser had barely come to a stop when Dangelo flung the door open and jumped from the car, sprinting to the entrance of the Acme Toy Company. The door with the crazy clown lettering was open.

Dangelo climbed the narrow stairwell two steps at a time, while Peggy Marshall and officer O'Shaughnessy tried to keep up. Shredded paper littered the stairs. Thumbtacks held the torn remnants of posters ripped off the walls.

The Acme Toy Company was no more. Desks had been wiped clean except for the telephones. Any trace of what went on in that room had been removed in a hurry, as evidenced by the empty manila file folders littering the floor.

"According to my contact," Marshall explained apologetically, "this was a beehive of activity less than 24 hours ago. They were tipped off!"

Dangelo gave her a disgusted look. "Yeah, well, there's nothing here now. Let's get back to headquarters."

• • •

The Mercedes hearse looked as long and black as death as Herman pulled up in front of San Pedro Plastics Laboratories. Johann looked up one side of Beacon Street and down the other. The coast was clear, but there was always a chance cops might still inside the warehouse. They entered through the service entrance in back of the building. They ripped off the crime scene tape and used a key to let themselves in.

"What luck!" Herman whooped. "Nobody home!"

The building was empty. Even better, the coffin was still there, perched on its sawhorses. The agents worked fast. Herman found a hand truck and slid it under the coffin.

"This place gives me the heebie jeebies," Johann grimaced, "even more than the funeral home."

"If you'd stop whining we'd get out of here sooner," Herman barked. "Give me a hand with this coffin!"

Wheeling the casket out the door onto the sidewalk, Johann began to unwind. To any bystander, they looked like two funeral home employees loading a coffin into a hearse; nothing odd about that. They pushed the Omega III onto the tiny steel rollers in the back of the Mercedes and slid it straight in.

Piling into the front seat, Herman pushed the starter and the Mercedes lurched forward in first gear. They were on their way to the Precision Tool Company. What they did not know was why.

The road had become so familiar, the two agents could have driven it blindfolded. But the wary eye of Gatekeeper saw plenty. He spotted the hearse barreling up the road and knew this was something Miss Laura should know about.

She thought I should know about it too, and looked for someone to take a message to me. She saw Jared playing Parcheesi with Rochelle in the lobby.

"Jared!" Borealis caterwauled from her office. "Be a good boy and run up to Miss Paloma's cabin. Tell her I want to see her right away!"

"Sure thing, Miss Laura, as long as Rochelle doesn't mind waiting for me."

"Of course I'll wait, Jared," Rochelle replied. "I'm winning."

Not wanting to lose a moment with the nubile Rochelle, Jared sprinted to my cabin in a flash. He knocked ferociously on the screen door.

"Miss Laura says she wants to see you right away, Miss Paloma!" Jared wheezed, catching his breath.

I went to the porch and called out to Dick in his cabin, and the three of us walked briskly down to the lodge. We found Miss Laura waiting behind the massive redwood slab that served as the front desk.

"Gatekeeper asked me to tell you about a hearse driving up the road lickity-split. He said it looked like the same two galoots that have given you youngsters so much grief lately; you know, the ones who hurt Rochelle."

"That means they're going to the warehouse," I replied. "This time they won't get away! Come on, Dick, and bring your .32."

We dashed back to our cabins, dressed, and climbed into Dick's Pontiac. Miss Laura had ordered Gatekeeper down to the gate so we wouldn't have to wait as we always do. Within minutes we were driving up the narrow fire road to the Precision Tool Company warehouse.

Dick parked the Pontiac far enough down the road so the feds wouldn't hear us coming. As before, we'd surprise them. Taking the car was a lot easier than climbing Karswell Falls to get here.

Reaching the warehouse on foot, we hopped over the brick wall and snuck a peek through a window. That's when we saw our prey. They were hefting Karswell's Omega III onto a pair of sawhorses.

"That must be the real Omega III, Dick," I whispered. "They must have brought it from San Pedro. Why'd they bring it all the way up here?"

"Beats me, but now's our chance to nail these creeps for the last time."

"You don't know how happy that will make me," I growled. "I owe them one for the dress I ruined in that tar pit."

The creeps still hadn't learned to lock the front door, so we let ourselves in and tiptoed through the front office to the door leading into the back room. As Dick reached for the doorknob, the wall phone began clanging like a four alarm fire alarm. It must have been one of those extra loud warehouse bells made to be heard throughout the building. We dashed back outside before someone answered it. One of them did.

"Yes, it's here," we heard him say. "You're coming up? Okay, we'll be here, no problem. No, we won't let anything happen to the casket."

He hung up the receiver and disappeared into the back room. This new information changed our plan. If we waited long enough, we'd corral the big cheese and his two flunkies in one swoop. I wanted the big boss even more than his two gunsels.

"Let's not tip our hand just yet, Dick. When Mr. Big gets here, we'll nab all three. We'd better move your car off the road where no one can see it."

A little voice in my head scolded me for not calling Peggy Marshall for backup. Once Mr. Big arrived, we would be outnumbered. I kept that thought to myself as Dick drove his car farther off the road, camouflaging it behind trees and brush. From there we walked back to the warehouse to settle into our hiding place where we waited in silence.

The crunching sound of tires on gravel told us a car was heading our way. A black Buick sedan lurched to a stop with a cloaked figure behind the wheel. From our hideaway we clearly saw the driver of the car. The Crystal Ball Killer, dressed in his iconic black hood and robes, climbed out of the Buick and strode into the warehouse, slamming the door behind him.

"What's he doing here?" I wondered out loud.

"We can take a wild guess," Dick replied. "Peggy said the killer escaped the police raid, didn't she? First the coffin shows up and now him. He wants that Omega III."

Dick reached into his pocket for the reassuring feel of his pistol. It felt smaller than he remembered it.

"Let's see what they're up to," I whispered. "If we can't surprise them, our goose is cooked."

CHAPTER 24

**S**taring through a shroud of cobwebs at the window, we focused on three figures near the coffin. The killer stood behind it, speaking to his henchmen. So this was the big boss man in charge of Operation Phoenix. I found a small piece of rusted steel plate on the ground and used it to pry the window. It opened just enough to listen to what was being said inside.

The robed figure removed his hood and wiped his forehead with a handkerchief. We got a good look at him, and it could only be — Brace Moreland! He wore a crew cut, tortoise shell glasses, and was clean-shaven. He looked more like a librarian that a serial killer, and he was sweating profusely. He was nervous, agitated. He wanted out of there, fast.

"We had no idea," Herman said, "you were the guy that iced those fortunetellers, boss."

"Why would you, unless I told you?" Moreland growled. "All I want from you is to connect this coffin to the power grid in this building. I'll need a large jolt of electricity to reach the year 1968."

"W-what?" Johann stammered. "You mean it's true? That thing really can take you to the future?"

"Not that it's any of your concern, but time travel is the whole point of having a time machine isn't it? Now, get moving!"

It surprised us as much as his gunsels. Brace Moreland and the Crystal Ball Killer were one and the same. And now that we had compromised Project Phoenix, he had to leave town; not just Los Angeles, but from the year 1951. He would exist 18 years in the future, where not even the LAPD had an arm long enough to catch him.

The two feds hustled about the warehouse looking for electrical hook-ups and cords that might work with the Omega III. Moreland opened the casket and began adjusting knobs inside. He was setting the controls for a trip to 1968.

Close to Dick's ear, I said: "If we don't make our move soon, we'll miss our chance. I don't know if time travel is real or not, but he seems to think it is, and so do the feds. Maybe there's something to it."

Dick whispered back: "We'd better get the drop on them while they're working on that coffin."

I said: "Okay, Dick, it's now or never. Let's go!"

We snuck around the corner to the front of the warehouse and padded into the office. I couldn't help but wonder if we could pull this stunt a second time. Now inside the back room, we hid behind a stack of coffins.

"Can't you two move any faster?" Moreland barked. "Where's that cable?"

"This joint isn't set up for this kind of work," one of them said. "We'll have to jerry-rig the coffin with what we got."

"Then do it! I haven't got all day!"

Moreland pushed a button on the end of the coffin. A small door popped open revealing an electrical socket. Johann yanked a heavy power cable from Karswell's Crematron vending machine and attached it to a power control panel. He plugged the other end into the coffin.

As the three men focused intently on their work, we jumped out from behind the coffins and Dick aimed his .32 at Moreland.

"Hold it right there!" Dick shouted. "All three of you, turn around and face the wall. Paloma, get that rope over there and tie them up. I don't want a repeat of the last time we did this."

"My pleasure," I said. "But first, I have something to say to the lederhosen boys.

As I approached, one of them twitched, as if he were about to spin around and sock me. I took him out with a chop to his jugular. He went down. Then I walloped the other chump and he went down too.

"That made my job a little easier," I said. "Now there's only you, Moreland. Or do you prefer Crystal Ball Killer?"

"I have no name, Miss Liu. As far as you and the LAPD are concerned, I don't exist. I'll be going now, and I'm taking the Omega III with me."

"You're pretty confident for someone who's got a gun aimed at his bread basket," I said.

"Yes, I am." Moreland pushed his knee against a button on the Omega III. A bolt of electricity shot in my direction, knocking me to the floor. When Dick turned his attention to me, Moreland grabbed a crowbar on top of the coffin and threw it at Dick's revolver, knocking it out of his hand. Before Dick knew it, Moreland had me in his clutches, a knife at my throat.

"You wouldn't want something unpleasant to happen to Miss Liu, would you, Barnett? Now, kick that gun against the wall and step over here!"

The jig was up and Dick knew it. He did as he was told, walking slowly toward the coffin. I was coming to, but I ached all over. I felt like I'd stuck my entire body into an electrical socket. As Dick came closer Moreland pulled a fast one.

"Take her!" he roared, and shoved me at Dick. He grabbed me before I hit the floor.

"You two have been a thorn in my side far too long," Moreland growled. "And I don't plan on meeting you in another 18 years, especially now that you know my identity. Therefore, you must die."

"Those two over there know who you are," Dick said, pointing his chin at the chumps I put to sleep.

"They won't talk," Moreland said. "And even if they did, who would believe a story about a time traveling serial killer? Sounds kind of crazy, even to me. All they'd get for their story is a straight jacket with three hots and a cot."

"Maybe yes, and maybe no," a familiar voice croaked.

Standing behind Moreland was Gatekeeper, holding a length of two-by-four above the killer's head. He brought it down and conked Moreland on the cranium. Moreland kissed the floor goodnight.

"Gatekeeper?" Dick gulped. "How, I mean, where'd you come from?"

"Well, I got to thinkin' 'bout those two n'er-do-wells on the floor over there. They looked like trouble when I saw 'em headin' up the road. But when I saw the Buick with this hooded hooligan drivin' like the devil himself was after him, I thought you might need some help."

Dick retrieved his revolver from the floor.

"Gatekeeper, your timing was perfect. Help me tie these three creeps up while we wait for the cops."

I dashed to the office phone and began dialing. I called Peggy Marshall first, since she had her own contacts at the LAPD. She picked up right away.

"Peggy," I yelped. "We've got the Crystal Ball Killer. Brace Moreland and the killer are one and the same. Call your LAPD friend and get a squad car up to the Precision Tool Company warehouse fast. I think you've got your big story!"

Peggy said she would call Lt. Dangelo. Once she knew the cops were on their way she would take her car and meet us here.

By my calculation, it would take the bulls less than an hour to get here. Dick kept our prisoners covered with his .32 and Gatekeeper looked pretty tough with his two-by-four. Forty minutes later we heard the sound of automobiles out front. I began to unwind.

Car doors slammed, footfalls headed our way. The warehouse door crashed open. A half dozen men in dark suits, guns drawn entered the room. The badges hanging from their breast pockets said FBI.

CHAPTER 25

o doubt about it, they were feds, and they were aiming their Government .45s directly at Dick.

"Okay, junior, drop the pea shooter!" their mouthpiece barked.

Dick let go of his snub nose like it was on fire. One of the agents came over, picked it up, and stuffed it into his coat pocket.

"Now, you two, move over there," the fed yapped, pointing at me and Gatekeeper. He herded us a safe distance from the coffin. Another fed knelt over Moreland, attempting to bring him to. Two others attended to Johann and Herman, untying them, standing them on their feet. Cursing, the gunsels brushed off the sawdust they acquired from the floor.

I was too angry to hold my tongue. To the man in charge I said: "I should have known you tapped the warehouse phone. My mistake."

"What we do is none of your concern," the G-man grated. "If you'd kept your nose out of our business you wouldn't be on the receiving end of this gun."

"Since when did taking a serial killer off the streets become a crime? Does J. Edgar know what you're up to, or did he think up Project Phoenix all by himself?"

"Like I said, what we do is none of your concern."

I knew I should keep my mouth shut, but our goose was already cooked, so what difference would it make?

"Who writes your material, Lex Luther?" I jabbed.

"I'm afraid you've become a liability to our government. America won't miss the likes of two Socialists like you and your nudist boyfriend over there. Deportation is far too complicated. We have a better way."

The fed patting Moreland's mug was having some luck. Gatekeeper must have given him a real wallop. The knocked-out nimrod's eyelids began to flutter. Moreland shook his head like a wet Doberman, but his devious mind was already hard at work. Unsteadily, he stood up.

"Karswell Falls is beyond the woods out back," Moreland explained, pointing through a rear window. "Take them to the falls and throw them over. It'll look like an unfortunate hiking accident. Even if it doesn't, no one will suspect us."

My mind was racing. I wondered what a red-blooded heroine in a movie matinee say at a time like this?

"You'll never get away with it! The cops will be here any minute!"

Then the bad guy would say, "That's as old as grandpa's mustache cup."

So, I kept my mouth shut.

"Get moving!" the G-man ordered, pointing his roscoe in our direction. He waved it toward the rear of the building. We moved.

Two feds escorted us into the woods. After traipsing through underbrush for what seemed like forever, it became apparent they had no idea where Karswell Falls was. They assumed we knew where we were going. Instead, we were meandering in erratic circles, buying time until the cavalry arrived. Lucky for us it finally did.

Three LAPD cruisers pulled up in front of Precision Tool Company. Car doors flew open as ten harness bulls piled out, with Lt. Dangelo leading the charge. But Dangelo mistakenly thought we had the situation under control. He was in for a surprise.

As soon as they entered the warehouse, the feds opened up on them. The bulls returned fire with a vengeance, remembering their San Pedro lab debacle. One of the feds went down, and the others put their hands in the air.

"I'm a federal agent!" the leader yeeped.

"Yeah, yeah, I've heard that one before," Dangelo growled. "Keep 'em up and you won't get drilled. Where's the girl PI? C'mon, let's have it. What'd you do with her?"

Now that the jig was up, the fed knew that throwing us over the falls might not be such a good idea.

"They're in the woods, heading to Karswell Falls. Two agents are with them, so don't open fire."

Dangelo grated through his grinders: "That depends on them, doesn't it? I haven't forgotten how your boys punctured one of our finest back in San Pedro.

"Connelly! You and Spillane get out there and track 'em down. No telling how far they've got by now. If they give you any trouble, you know what to do. Just don't hit the innocent bystanders."

Peggy Marshall pulled her Studebaker up behind the squad cars and dashed into the warehouse. Seeing Dangelo, she yelped:

"Where's Paloma and Dick?"

"Somewhere in those woods," he replied, "heading to the falls with two feds."

Without another word, Peggy ran out the rear door into the woods. She began calling my name. It was faint, but I heard. So did the two G-men. They stopped and listened.

"What do you think?" one said to the other. "Should we wait here and nab her, too?"

"We'd better wait," the other one agreed, then called out: "Over here!"

That alerted the two harness bulls traipsing through the underbrush, which was good luck for us, but not so much for the G-men. The bulls were first to spot us.

"Hold it right there, you two!" Connelly shouted. "Drop your weapons and you won't get hurt."

That's when lead pills began flying faster than yellow jackets at an Oddfellows' picnic. First the feds began firing, then the cops. We hit the ground and stayed there. The gunfire roused Dangelo, who sent two more cops into the woods. They took positions behind nearby trees and began firing at the feds, who were now caught in a crossfire. The feds were outnumbered.

They threw out their weapons and came out from behind the trees, hands in the air. That's when we stood up and waved to the cops. Next thing I knew, Peggy Marshall was running up to us.

"I had no idea you were in so much trouble, Paloma!" she gasped. "You didn't tell me the feds were here."

"They weren't until 20 minutes ago. They tapped the warehouse phone and heard everything we said. Everything was under control until they showed up."

Dangelo's men cuffed the two agents and took them to Dangelo.

"Okay, here we go again." Dangelo said. "Who's got the guy with the hood?"

"These are the only two we found, sir," Spillane replied.

"Where in H is he now?" Dangelo griped. "Find him! He's got to be in this warehouse!"

No sooner had Dangelo's minions begun their search when we heard a strange crackling hum. It came from the Omega III, already prepped for Moreland's escape. During the mêlée, Moreland had slipped into the coffin unnoticed. Bolts of electricity came out of a misty, green fog engulfing the coffin.

"Spillane!" Dangelo squawked, "Don't let him get away!"

Spillane rushed the coffin and was swallowed up in the green fog. The cop was lifted a few feet into the air, then fell paralyzed onto the floor. Spillane was proof that a deadly electrical force surrounded the Omega III. No one could stop Moreland now.

We backed away and watched the green fog glow red, violet, then, poof! Moreland, the Crystal Ball Killer, was no more. The Omega III went with him, leaving empty sawhorses.

The Incredible Karswell would not be pleased when I gave him my final report — and my bill. Dangelo was even less pleased.

"Dammit all to hades!" he spat. "We lost him again!"

"Lieutenant," I uttered, "If what Moreland said was true, he's transported himself to the San Francisco Bay Area to the year 1968."

"All I know is, he's left me with an open case," Dangelo groaned. "and I hate open cases! These guys," he said, pointing to the G-men, "are no good to me. They'll get sprung as soon as the big boys find out we've got 'em."

And so, the day ended as it began, without resolution. Karswell would never see his grandfather's coffin, the LAPD would not have their murder suspect, and Peggy Marshall would be denied the story she had hoped for.

On the other hand, I still had two days of unused vacation, and was determined to have as much fun as possible.

Peggy, Dick, Gatekeeper, and I watched as the cops hauled off the G-men. Frowning, Dangelo slammed the door of his police cruiser and drove off down the mountain road.

Gatekeeper finally broke the silence: "I better get back to camp, Counselor Dick. I'll leave the gate unlocked so you two can let yourselves in," he said. "I'll trust you to put the chain and lock back once you're inside." We promised we would.

"I'm heading back to the office," Peggy said dejectedly. "I'm not quite sure how to report the ending of this story. Without Moreland in custody — in fact, not even in existence — how do I explain what just happened? That he was a time traveling serial killer who escaped in a time machine? Who'd believe that? I'll lose all credibility as a crime reporter."

"That's what Moreland and the feds were counting on," Dick replied. "They knew their plan was so outlandish that even if they were found out, they could deride it as too fantastic to be real."

Peggy thought about what Dick just said. "And what better way for a killer to escape justice than to be someone who doesn't exist? The Crystal Ball Killer didn't even know his victims and had no record in 1951. By using Moreland, the feds thought they'd keep a lid on Operation Phoenix. No telling what they really wanted to do with that coffin."

"I guess we'll never know," I said cheerily. "But I've got two vacation days left, and I'm going to enjoy every minute of them."

CHAPTER 26

he nudist life is a great life. I woke up safe and sound the next morning in Jaybird Cottage, listening to the distant clang of the breakfast bell. That meant Dick would be here shortly. I lingered a while longer in bed, waiting for him to magically appear like he did on my first day at Sunland.

Dick's penchant for promptness meant I didn't have to wait long. Right on the dot, he yanked off my covers as I pretended sleep.

"C'mon, kiddo! You're burning daylight!!"

I yawned. "Oh, it's you, Dick. Is something wrong?"

"Who'd you think it was? It's time for breakfast."

"I don't know, Dick. Maybe I'll sleep in today."

"I brought the sun tan oil."

"On second thought, I do feel a bit peckish."

I put my feet on the floor, stretched my arms above my head and wiggled the girls to wake them up. Dick poured a generous amount of oil into his hand and began rubbing his hands together vigorously.

I asked: "Where do I need it most?"

"You look pale all over to me, so, stand up." he said, massaging my shoulders. "You didn't put in enough time sunbathing to fade those tan lines."

Feeling less hungry than aroused, I purred: "It's not like I didn't want to. Why don't we just skip breakfast today?"

"Heck, no! We're still on vacation. We'll have plenty of time for that after we eat."

"Not today we won't."

"What do you mean?"

"I have to give my final report to Karswell. I'm meeting him after breakfast. Miss Laura said he'd be here today to give a short lecture to the group. He's staying at the lodge. As you know, that's a rare occasion."

We arrived at the Mess Hall and dove into the sea of bare bodies; very tanned bare bodies. Bob and Frank were in their usual spot, as was Edwina and Chick. Lively Rochelle served meals, but today the

Bandaids on her shoulders and arms were gone. Dark red splotches marked her skin, a grim reminder of Operation Phoenix.

"Why, Dick! Paloma! Welcome back!" Rochelle chirped, holding our tofu scrambles under her freckled breasts.

"This time I won't ask."

"Ask what?"

"Where you've been."

"Hardly worth a mention," Dick crooned. "We were taking care of some business among the textiles, that's all."

"Business, huh? Whatever you say, Dick. Here's your scramble and some toast, gluten free, of course."

She laid out our meals. The toast came on two smaller plates — far too small for me! I hadn't eaten in 24 hours, nor had Dick. Tofu never tasted so good, not even back home in Chinatown. Rochelle watched me wolf down my scramble, went back to the kitchen and brought out seconds. Eating was a great way to stall for time, too. I wasn't looking forward to my chat with Karswell. Dick sat and watched as I ravaged two meals.

"When you've had enough to eat," he said, "what do you say we go for a sail? It's a perfect day for it. There's a nice breeze."

I shoved the last corner of toast into my mouth. Chewing, I mumbled: "Remember? I've got an appointment with Karswell. I have his fee, too. That's the important part. You know I'd rather spend time with you on the lake, Dick, but business is business, even here."

"If the wind holds," he said, "an evening sail might even be better."

The hall was atwitter over Karswell's approaching lecture. Everyone had seen the notice on the bulletin board: "Is the World Ready to Get Naked? A lecture by The Incredible Karswell! In person! Remain in your seats after breakfast!"

This put the crowd in a jolly mood. Instead of bolting outside to frolic on the volleyball court, they waited patiently until the appointed time when Karswell would appear on stage. Most of the guests had never seen him as a fellow nudist, only as a Hollywood personality on television.

Finally, from stage left, Jerome Karswell, wearing nothing but his Birkenstock sandals, strolled to the podium. Behind him stood the official Sunland flag: a big letter "S" superimposed over the sun's rays. Karswell tapped the microphone a few times with his finger to call the room to attention.

"Testing, testing, one, two, three," he intoned in his famous sepulchral voice. "Can you hear me out there?"

A resounding "YES!" followed by applause rose from the crowd.

"Very well, then." Karswell began. "My fellow nudists, whether you realize it or not, you are brave soldiers in a movement that will conquer the suppression of Man's deepest yearnings as human beings. That movement, my friends, is called nudism.

"Maybe you joined the movement because you felt disconnected from the world around you. The textiles that confined your body oppressed you. You were living a lie and you knew it. Yes, that may have been the reason you joined.

"Then again, maybe you came to nudism for health reasons. Many of us do so. Physicians have given learned medical explanations of the benefits of the sun's rays on naked skin, in terms of vitamins and ultra-violet light. Yes, the sun will banish our prisoner's pallor and bestow strength in our bones and courage in our hearts.

"Yes, my friends, nudism connects us to our ancient star, Sol in an elemental form of worship. The stress and strain of daily life, with its pretentious posing and exaggerated fears, have isolated too many of us. But, all that is cast aside here at Sunland.

"Naked, and naked only, do we know who our brothers and sisters are, and that Earth, our Great Mother, is our nourishing mother still.

"As the old painters knew, there is beauty in the naked human form, from cradle to old age. The misguided notion that only youth is beautiful is banished by nakedness and sunshine. In a dazzling flash, one learns the worth of every human being when we are naked."

With rapt attention on Karswell's hypnotic voice, the crowd looked as if mesmerized. With a sip of mountain spring water, he continued.

"There are seven colors in the sun's rays whose wave-lengths our bodies need, both men and women. Inside our clothing we barely get enough of these rays to stay alive. We all know how we feel in wintertime, when we're wearing bulky winter clothing. We become moody, down, depressed. Why? Because we don't get enough sun, that's why! Ask any doctor and he'll tell you.

"In closing, my friends, let me just say this. It has never been from the land of snow and ice that great religious prophets emerge, but from the lands where nakedness goes unmolested, and the sun shines bright and hot. No pagan Christ ever wore furs."

With that, Karswell exited the stage to thunderous applause.

I turned to Dick: "He's on his way to the lodge," I groaned. "I'd better get this over with."

I left the hall, returning to Jaybird Cottage to put on my Chinese jade necklace and collect my invoice for services rendered. I checked myself in the mirror: cartwheel hat, sunglasses, necklace. Yes, these three items had become my signature "look" at Sunland. I was ready to face The Incredible Karswell.

As I walked down to the lodge I ran into Gatekeeper. There had always been something that confused me about him. He was never naked, always in his textiles. He looked like a farmer in a sea captain's hat.

"Hello, there, Miss," Gatekeeper coughed as I stopped in front of him. "You're back to your old self again, I see."

"It sure feels like it," I echoed. "Gatekeeper, I've always wondered why you never take off your textiles here? Don't you enjoy the nudist lifestyle?"

"Ha! I know I don't conform to the nudist lifestyle, Miss. But as the gatekeeper and caretaker here, I intend to look the part. People recognize me like this. If I were naked like all of you, I wouldn't look like Gatekeeper and it'd be harder to find me when you needed me. It's easy for anyone to know where I am, dressed like this."

"Makes sense," I said. "I was just curious. By the way, thanks for helping us out of our jam yesterday."

"My pleasure, Miss. Part of my job is to keep you guests safe."

I continued on. The camp's golf cart was heading my way with Laura Borealis at the helm. The smoking, churning machine sputtered to a stop alongside me.

"Jerome sent me to pick you up, Miss Paloma," she said. "He's anxious to hear the outcome of the case."

"I'm not anxious to tell him about it, but I'd be happy to ride the rest of the way."

Jerome Karswell rocked compulsively in the lobby rocking chair. Seeing Karswell naked was still disconcerting. I was not sure why, since we were all naked here. His pasty-white skin belied the notion that he spent time basking naked under our glorious star, Sol. More than likely he spent all his time schmoozing at Hollywood parties. Those floral boxer shorts he wore at his Bunker Hill apartment gave much needed color to his otherwise vapid complexion.

"Ah, Miss Liu, I've been waiting for you," Karswell chimed like a church bell. "What kept you? Oh, never mind that. What's the status of my coffin? Did you find it?"

"Yes, I found it," I said.

"Wonderful! Where is it?"

"It has ceased to exist. At least, in the year 1951."

"I do not like the sound of this, Miss Liu, whatever it is you're trying to tell me. What do you mean it has ceased to exist in 1951?"

I gave it to him straight, the whole ball of wax: Project Phoenix, the time machine in his grandfather's coffin, the feds, the Crystal Ball Killer, the tar pits, and the scene at Precision Tools where his beloved casket vanished along with his erstwhile manager, Brace Moreland.

I wrapped it up with: "Not only was Brace Moreland part of Project Phoenix, he was also the Crystal Ball Killer. But what I would like to know, Mr. Karswell, is how you managed to hire him?"

"He had spotless credentials as I recall," Karswell said, tepidly. "I received his resume in the mail a few days after grandfather Karswell passed. I invited him for an interview, it was that simple. Now that I think about it, he was extremely interested in grandfather's coffin. Now I understand why."

I gave my handwritten invoice to Karswell, who looked surprised as he read it.

"That's for ten days at $25 per day, plus expenses," I explained. "And it includes a new dress. Mine was ruined when I was pushed into the La Brea Tar Pits."

"Three hundred and sixty-seven dollars and fifty cents?" Karswell sputtered. "And I didn't even get my Omega III back?"

"Included in that fee are the two attempts on my life, Mr. Karswell. I'd say it's a bargain. Eighteen years from now I can try to locate your coffin in 1968. By then it'll be closer to my home office in San Francisco."

Miss Laura elbowed Karswell's side.

"Pay her, Jerome! She put her life on the line, even if you didn't get your coffin back. She deserves every penny."

"Very well, but I'm paying under duress." Karswell clomped into the office on his cork-soled sandals to dig up his checkbook. I know nudist culture is all about the acceptance of all body types, but Karswell looked a lot more incredible in glittery clothing. He returned, check in hand. I thanked him, said my goodbyes, and returned to Jaybird Cottage where I hoped to find Dick waiting for me.

The cabin was empty, but I found him next door. I pulled his screen door open and walked in. He was lounging in his easy chair, reading. I waved Karswell's check in the air.

"He was a skinflint, but he paid!" I yodeled. "Next bottle of sun tan oil is on me, or dinner in Pasadena, your choice. I still have some worry-free vacation time left, so, where were we? Yes, now I remember. You were lubing my mounded enticements with sun tan oil. Where's that bottle?"

CHAPTER 27

he sun rose sadly on the penultimate day of my vacation. By late afternoon Dick and I were relaxing on a plaid blanket at the nude beach Peggy Marshall told me about. In fact, Peggy came with us. She showed us the best spot to spread our blanket and hoist the umbrella. She even brought a picnic basket with sandwiches.

Dick had parked his car on the Pacific Coast Highway. From there we hiked through an arroyo for a quarter of a mile. The trail became a meandering, but well traveled path surrounded by beach grass until the blue horizon of the Pacific Ocean loomed ahead of us. Naked people frolicked in the waves along the beach.

We made camp next to a sand dune to block the offshore breeze; a Santa Ana, Dick called it. Once the blankets were down, we got naked.

"You can barely see your tan lines, Paloma," Dick observed. "I think you've almost caught up with us."

"Yeah, right. You can't fool me, Dick," i replied. "They were there this morning when I looked in the mirror. Anyway, I'll get them all back again as soon as I hit the fog in San Francisco. It'll be a tough adjustment putting on the wool outfit I wear around the office."

"Don't think about that now," Peggy said. "You'll have plenty of time for that on the drive home."

Even though I grew up in the delta, I had never skinny-dipped in the Sacramento River. That would have brought dishonor to my Chinese dad. But today was the day I would hit the ocean waves in the nude.

Peggy had turned in her final story on the Crystal Ball Killer, but it wasn't the story she had hoped for. J. Edgar Hoover himself contacted her editor, putting the fear of God into him if any mention of Project Phoenix appeared in his newspaper. Hoover must have had the same chat with the LAPD, because the lid came down hard on any more information from them. A lawyer with a writ of Habeas Corpus appeared at the Los Angeles City Hall after Dangelo booked the G-men he'd rounded up at Precision Tool. All records of the booking went to the shredder.

Peggy had to rewrite her story. Instead, she focused on the killer's last victim, Ivy Wyldwind and her Siamese cat, Madame Blavatsky. The headline read: "Murder Victim's Orphaned Cat Seeks New Home." The editor buried the story on page six of the bulldog edition in the Sunday paper.

Peggy said she received half a dozen calls from readers, all hoping to adopt the cat. One caller, a fortuneteller named Crystal Thorne from Venice Beach, became the cat's lucky new owner. It seemed only fitting.

"That was my story to end all stories," Peggy grumbled as she rubbed suntan oil on her taught thighs. "On the bright side, though, we're not undertaker bait like we could have been. Especially you, Paloma."

I nodded in agreement. "I still get a whiff of crude oil every now and then," I grimaced. "like it seeped into my pores."

Dick, his eyes closed, had been half listening. His legs were in the sun, his torso shaded by our oversized beach umbrella.

"Why don't you two hit the waves? This is what you've been waiting for, isn't it, Paloma? A nude swim in the ocean?"

We jumped up, sprinting to shore. I sank my feet into the wet sand and waded in. Treading farther out, the floor suddenly dropped out from under me and I dove under a wave. It was cold, but not as cold as the Yuba River when the Sierra snow pack melts.

"Jeez, Peggy! The water here is just as cold as Frisco!"

"You'll get used to it," she laughed. "Sometimes it warms up to 68 degrees."

I swam out as far as I dared. I knew about the Great Whites. We have them off Stinson Beach, near Bolinas. Peggy hung back, bobbing up and down in the waves. We'd been out for maybe half an hour when she saw Dick waving his arms for us to come back in.

"Paloma! Lunch!" Peggy yelled.

It felt as though the salt water had cleansed every pore in my body. Free of soggy swimsuits, we ran back to our blankets, where Dick had laid out our meal. He was opening a bottle of Paso Robles wine as we sat down.

From under our umbrella we watched the sun set. We packed our leftovers in Peggy's wicker basket, and began searching through the pile of textiles for our clothes. Hunting for his boxer shorts, Dick found our bras, which he handed over to us. Packed and dressed, we hiked the narrow path back to Dick's Pontiac.

Did I mention Dick's car was equipped with a phone under the dash? He uses it to stay in touch with the office when he's at a job site. Peggy asked if she could call the *Times* switchboard to check for messages. From the strained look on her face, she had one.

"There's been another murder!" she announced. "A fortuneteller. She was one of the last two Inner Circle members. Bertha Langtree. That leaves Charlie Chan. He's the last man standing. I'd better call Lt. Dangelo and see what gives."

That put a dent in what had been a glorious day. I was officially off the Karswell case and had no desire to get dragged into another murder. Still, what did it mean for us? I thought we'd seen the last of the Crystal Ball Killer. We dropped Peggy at the *Times* and headed back up the mountain to Sunland, riding in silence. What was there to say? All the old angst was coming back.

After the usual 20-minute wait, Gatekeeper met us at the gate. Safely back in Dick's cabin we stripped off our clothes, but that didn't help our mood. I suggested an oiling session might help. It knew would help me, but Dick thought a sail on the lake might sharpen our wits. Begrudgingly, I agreed.

At the lake we walked to the end of the pier and boarded the camp sailboat. Dick checked the charge on the battery before untying us from

There's been another murder!

the pier. The sail fluttered as it caught the evening breeze. Gliding along, we came to terms with our situation.

"What do you think, Paloma?" Dick frowned. "Should we stay out of this, or is it something we need to follow through?"

"Honestly, I'd like to spend the last day of vacation clothing free, Dick, but maybe we should talk it over with Peggy. I don't see why the killer would keep knocking people off, now that so many others know about the Omega III."

"Then why this last murder, if not to keep Bertha Langtree quiet?" Dick replied.

"We're back to square one," I sighed. "I'm just not seeing the point of all this."

"On the other hand, does this mean we're still in trouble?" Dick wondered. "Do we need to get him before he gets us?"

My stomach growled.

"I'm hungry," I said. "Let's get to the Mess Hall before we miss dinner. Besides, it's getting chilly out here."

Since this was our last dinner of the season, Naked Chef made a special dessert: chocolate tofu cheese cake with a toasted coconut crust. After supper we returned to Dick's cabin, where my one-track mind still saw Dick as what my vacation was all about. After an hour of mutual admiration, we laid back on Dick's bed, pondering our next move. About the killer, I mean.

"What about a trip to Chinatown?" Dick suggested. "The last domino to fall, should be Charlie Chan, right? After J. Edgar warned everyone off, I bet the cops don't even have him staked out. Maybe we should go find out."

The thought of donning my panty girdle and Permalift had little appeal. The grooves they make in my flesh take too long to disappear. But, I was willing to trade discomfort for resolution.

"Maybe you're right," I said, wiping sweat from my chest. "I suppose it wouldn't hurt to have a talk with him. But first, I need a shower."

"Mine or yours?"

"Mine," I said. "My street clothes are next door."

Back in Jaybird Cottage, I showered, toweled off, and began the tedious ritual called "getting dressed." I rolled my gunmetal gray hose up my thighs and hooked them onto my panty girdle. I stuffed my 34Ds into the Permalift, zipped up my skirt, and was ready to head back down the mountain.

Dick was outside, leaning against his car, waiting for me. Guys have much less complicated clothing to put on.

"Gatekeeper must be getting tired of us coming and going like this," Dick said. "Most guests don't leave camp until vacation is over."

I said: "Let's have Miss Laura page him. He can ride to the gate with us. That way he won't have to walk."

Dick drove to the lodge, parked out front. We climbed the stairs to the lobby and stopped at the front desk, where Laura Borealis was checking the pigeonhole mailboxes behind the counter for unclaimed guest mail. She turned to us and looked surprised.

"Dick! Paloma! You're hiding inside those, those, textiles! I hardly recognized you. You're leaving again?"

"Yes, but we'll be back," I said. "Would you mind paging Gatekeeper? We'll give him a ride to the gate."

Gatekeeper arrived at the lodge, and we climbed into Dick's car. After a dusty drive down the dirt road we stopped at the gate. Gatekeeper pulled out his key ring and unlocked it. We passed through and we were on our way to the valley of textiles.

Taking Broadway in downtown LA, we passed the Bradbury Building, which was across the street from the Million Dollar Theater. I had been on vacation for two weeks and still hadn't done any sightseeing! I wanted to visit Grand Central Market, but no stopping there. We had business in Chinatown.

Broadway became North Broadway and from there Dick turned left on Ord. That took us directly into Chinatown. We parked a discrete distance from the Lucky You Gift Shop, Chan's store and walked the rest of the way.

There we found Charlie Chan stocking shelves with Hell Money behind the counter.

"Mr. Chan?" I said.

"Yes?"

"My name is Liu Tsong, a friend of Peggy Marshall. This is Dick Barnett. I'm a private investigator, working on the Crystal Ball Killer case with Peggy. We heard about the murder of Bertha Langtree. Not counting you, she was the last of the Inner Circle members. We got worried about your safety."

"So nice to concern yourself about this humble magician. But, fear not. I am safe here with my parrot, Li Po."

"You do realize you're the last Inner Circle member that hasn't been murdered," Dick said. "The odds are not in your favor you'll stay that way, even if you're careful. Why haven't the police put a guard on your front door?"

"Chan have no idea," he said. "In any case, would tell them not to bother. Chan protects self. Has secret weapon."

"Secret weapon?" I queried. "What do you mean?"

As if to explain, Chan went to the front door, flipped the OPEN sign to CLOSED, pulled down the shade. "Come with me."

He parted curtains behind the counter and we entered a room with an aroma of joss sticks and lotus flowers. Red silk Chinese lanterns hung from the ceiling, giving the room an eerie glow. Chan sat behind his desk and bade us to sit.

"Chan has heard of your exploits regarding Crystal Ball Killer and am most impressed. You were hired by Incredible Karswell, yes?"

"His wife, actually. She wanted the return of Karswell's coffin, but it disappeared along with the killer, into the future we assume."

Chan said: "Then, you know secret of Omega III?"

"We saw it in operation," Dick replied.

"Yes, most unusual. Now, Chan show you something also unusual."

We watched, dumbfounded, as Chan began tugging at his chin. His face wrinkled in bizarre contortions. His chin came forward until his entire face peeled off in his hands. A mask! This was no Chinese magician; he was a white man. And now, without Chan's face, the man's speech changed too.

"Pardon my theatrics," the man said. "I haven't taken this off in front of anyone until now, but it seemed like an appropriate time. Let me introduce myself. My name is Cranston Karswell."

His chin pulled forward until his entire face came off in his hands.

CHAPTER 28

ranston Karswell?" I croaked. "Jerome Karswell's grandfather?"

"Yes, Jerome is my grandson. He's a n'er do well, but my progeny nonetheless."

"But Jerome said he cremated you," I quavered.

"Indeed he did. But that was the Cranston Karswell of 1949, the year the coroner signed my death certificate. That's also when Jerome inherited my Omega III. He knew nothing of its capabilities, adding all sorts of gizmos, like his martini dispenser.

"However, I am Cranston Karswell of 1941. That was the year I developed the Omega III. As that Cranston Karswell, I am still very much alive. I have come here for personal reasons. As you have already learned, I was working with a group of like-minded metaphysicians to perfect the Omega III at that time. We had received the blueprint for it a few years prior, from Ashtar, an alien being living in another galaxy. Our original plan was to use it to return to 1918 Europe, when Adolf Hitler was a corporal in the German *Wermacht*. We wanted to make sure he didn't survive the war, which, as we saw it, would have nipped the Second World War in the bud."

"What happened?" I asked. "Hitler survived, and the war did happen."

"That was indeed unfortunate," Karswell griped. "Ashtar moved to another space/time continuum and we lost contact. Then, we ran into unanticipated problems that he, or she, whatever Ashtar was, could have cleared up for us. Left on our own, the bugs weren't worked out until after the war. By then I had other fish to fry."

Frowning, Dick said: "I don't understand this. How can you be cremated and still be here talking to us?"

Karswell, ignoring Dick's question, said: "I'm sure Jerome explained the family history to you, Miss Liu — about my fear of premature burial and all that malarkey?"

"Yes, he did. He said your fear of death is what made you invent the Omega III, 'For the person who isn't sure he's dead' — or something like that."

"Yes, that's what I told him, and he believed it, as he was meant to. I couldn't trust Jerome to keep his mouth shut about something as important as the Omega III. Loose lips sink ships, and Jerome's lips would sink the Queen Mary once they start flapping. I assume you've seen his television show?"

"Yes, I have. He does drone on. I suppose you knew the feds took Jerome's coffin and used it for what they called Project Phoenix. But to get here from 1941, you must have used the casket. How many Omega III's are there?"

"Technically only one," Karswell answered. "Theoretically, an infinite number."

"I still don't get it!" Dick said. "You're saying there are multiples of you AND the Omega III?"

"That's the beauty of time travel," Karswell grinned. "There are so many versions myself, I can sidestep my own death. Well, most of the time. The average person living in the 'now' would never realize this without an Omega III."

This new development added another wrinkle to the case. Not only was The Incredible Karswell's grandfather still alive, he had the original Omega III. And I had the feeling Cranston wouldn't let Jerome get his hands on it this time.

"If you don't mind telling us, Mr. Karswell," I said. "Why were you impersonating Charlie Chan?"

"Ah, yes, my Chan impersonation was a last minute decision," Cranston Karswell explained. "You see, I wanted to check on my grandson after I had, well, passed away, to see what he had done with the Omega III. When I saw the headlines about the murder of each member of my old Inner Circle, I thought I'd better stick around.

"I came to Charlie, who was quite surprised to see me, by the way, and volunteered to take his place, thus throwing the killer off his trail. He's staying with relatives up north. You see, Charlie used to work in the movie industry. He did Boris Karloff's makeup in some of those Universal horror films. Anyway, before Charlie left, he made this mask for me. An excellent likeness, don't you think?"

"It fooled me," Dick said.

Karswell's words were floating around the room. I was too busy thinking to hear them. We now had an Omega III. That could be useful, especially in the hands of its original owner.

"Mr. Karswell," I interrupted. "If the killer is still on a mission to murder every Inner Circle member, wouldn't Charlie Chan — you — be his last customer?"

Karswell thought before he spoke. He twisted one end of his mustache to a fine point with his thumb and forefinger, and said, "I'm afraid the killer's continued presence is due to my grandson's incompetence. Obviously, Jerome configured the circuitry incorrectly. It's my responsibility to make things right, so I plan to stop this madman. Charlie Chan, that is, Cranston Karswell, will be his final victim and his nemesis. I am the perfect bait for my trap."

Dick and I looked at one another, perplexed.

"In that case," I said, "how do you propose to stop him?"

"I'm still working on that part of the plan," he replied. "But as I recall, Charlie used to keep a loaded pistol in his cash drawer." Karswell went behind the small counter, opened a drawer, and brought out an ancient pistol. "Ah, yes, here it is. Problem solved."

"Okay, how about this?" I suggested. "While you get ready to confront the killer, we'll lay low on the other side of the plaza. Once we see him enter the shop, we'll come running. Don't worry. We won't be close enough that he'd see us."

It wasn't much of a plan, but it was the only one we had. Dick and I left the Lucky You and returned to Dick's Pontiac, scanning our surroundings the entire way. We saw no one. Dick slid behind the wheel, and I leaned back and relaxed on the passenger's side. We waited.

The dashboard clock said we'd been waiting for three hours already. If I was a smoker, I'd have quaffed a dozen cigarettes by now. Dick and I ran out of chitchat two hours ago, and the ticking of the dashboard clock seemed to get louder with every passing minute. Street traffic had vanished, the plaza was dead. No pedestrians traversed the sidewalks. Most of the garish neon signs with their colorful Chinese characters had flickered out long ago, leaving only a few street lamps glowing like worn out fireflies in the darkness.

"This may be a long stake out," I said. My voice roared like a canon shot in the silence. "For all we know, it could be days before Moreland shows up."

"True," Dick agreed. "And we're wasting valuable vacation time sitting here. We could be back at Sunland, playing tennis."

"It's three o'clock in the morning, Dick. You can't play tennis in the dark."

"Well, we could go for a nighttime skinny dip. The moon is full. Hold on! Somebody just slipped into that doorway over there."

"Where?"

"Over there, next to Hung Wei Low's chop suey joint. See him?"

A hooded figure hugged the wall, edging toward Charlie Chan's Lucky You Gift Shop.

"This is it, Dick! Have you got your .32 handy?"

"You bet, let's go!"

Dick had barely stuck his foot out the car door when two black Ford sedans with whip antennas screeched to a stop and dropped anchor in front of the gift shop. A dark panel truck brought up the rear. The sinister convoy blocked our view of the shop, and we lost sight of the hooded figure.

Several men in black suits converged on the shop. Two guards stood on either side of the front door. They brandished their weapons as they scanned the area.

We shrank down onto the front seat like deflating balloons.

I whispered: "This doesn't look good, Dick. Don't make a sound."

I glanced at the dash clock. Ten minutes had passed since the cars surrounded the shop. Slowly I edged my eyes above the windowsill. The front door to the shop opened and light poured out. Cranston Karswell emerged with a man on either side. They held his arms, escorting him to one of the black sedans.

Four other men emerged from the shop. They carried what looked like a large coffin — Karswell's Omega III, the original. They loaded it into the back of the panel truck and slammed the doors. The rumble of V-8 engines signaled the end of Cranston Karswell as the convoy sped off.

Dick exhaled. "Okay, Paloma. Let's get out of here."

"Not until we take a look inside the shop," I said.

"Look for what?"

"I don't know. Closure maybe. I just want to have a look."

Dick, as always, humored me. He punched the starter and drove the Pontiac toward the Lucky You Gift Shop with his headlights off. The plaza was as empty as a dead man's Monthly Planner.

He parked in front of the chop suey joint next to the Lucky You. We left the car doors slightly ajar so as not to make noise, then edged our way to the shop door. It was wide open. I'd brought my penlight and snapped it on. Inside, nothing seemed amiss, no broken furniture, just Karswell's Charlie Chan mask, lying on the counter.

We parted the curtains and entered the back room, where it seemed safe enough to turn on a light.

"I wonder how the feds knew Karswell was here?" Dick said.

In reply, a voice behind us squawked: "Put 'em up!"

We raised our hands slowly above our heads. Our goose was cooked yet again.

"Turn around!"

We turned, but saw no one. Preening herself on a perch in a corner of the room sat Li Po, Charlie's parrot.

"Jeez!" I yeeped. "It's just a parrot!"

"That bird belongs to the real Charlie Chan," Dick said. "I saw his act once. The parrot collects tips after the show. So, what now? Charlie's gone, and so's Karswell."

"I'll take her," I smiled. "Confidential Investigations needs a mascot."

Li Po hopped onto my arm and I put her into her cage. Dick carried her to the car. He wrestled the cage into the back seat and we were on our way back to Sunland. The sun was coming up over the San Gabriel Mountains as we reached Pasadena.

CHAPTER 29

Li Po squawked and whistled all the way to Sunland. It was a shrill whistle, too, the kind that shatters glass. By the time we reached Highland Park, Dick was ready to throw the bird out the window.

"She's just hungry," I said calmly. "She'll love the food at Sunland. Parrots like fruits and vegetables, don't they?

"All I know is, she'll be much happier in your cabin," Dick grumped. "She seems to like you. I'll bet she even speaks Chinese."

On reaching the Sunland gate, Dick pushed the horn ring on his steering wheel three times, and waited for Gatekeeper. There, our conversation took a somber turn.

"I can't believe we have to check out today," I said.

"I know," Dick groaned. "It's been one hell of a vacation."

"True, but from where I sit, I got paid, and free room and board."

"Paloma, have you ever thought about opening your own detective agency? I bet you'd do a land office business here in LA."

"I don't know, Dick. I'm a small town girl. I think I'm better off in my corner of San Francisco. That doesn't mean you can't come up to visit. I can show you around, maybe even take you up to the delta, where I grew up."

"I'll take you up on that," he said. "You know, a good architect can find work just about anywhere."

At that, Gatekeeper broke in. "Are you two back again?" I'd almost forgot you left, but here you are, big as life. It'll be a short stay, I'm afraid. Today's check out, you know."

"Far too short," I said. "It'll be back to the old grind and my work clothes."

"And I'll be closing down Sunland for the winter months," Gatekeeper replied. "It's a big job. Takes me nearly two months to get things ready for next season, especially when there's painting to do. Say, what's that in the back seat there?"

"It's a parrot," I replied. "She can't take her feathers off, not even for a nudist camp."

Gatekeeper snorted, "I don't reckon so, Miss. Okay, come on in. Miss Laura and Mr. Karswell are up at the lodge. You can say your goodbyes if you like.

"How about a lift back to the lodge?" Dick offered.

"Thanks, Counselor Dick, I don't mind the walk," Gatekeeper replied.

It was a bittersweet ride up the familiar pothole-strewn dirt road. Dick parked in front of his cabin. I pulled out Li Po from the back seat and carried her into my sitting room. She seemed happy to be inside and quieted down when I gave her a handful of sunflower seeds from the bowl I kept on the end table.

Then I stripped. It felt great to free myself again. My feminine underpinnings left their telltale grooves on my body, unpleasant reminders of the grip they held on our textile culture. Dick sauntered through the screen door, stripped down to his sandals.

"Ready to say goodbye to the Karswells?"

"Sure. Should we tell Jerome about his grandfather still being alive? I wonder if he'd even believe us?"

"He might. After all, he predicts the future, right?"

"Yeah, whatever."

Li Po squawked: "*Gung hay fah choy*! Gawk!"

"Did that parrot just say something in Chinese?" Dick grated. "What did it say?"

"She said congratulations and may you be prosperous," I translated. "But I think she just wants more seeds. I'll get some nuts out of the vending machine at the lodge. I'll be ready as soon as I put on my jade necklace. I'll expect one last application of sun tan oil before we go."

"Sorry, all out," Dick replied. "We used the last bottle at the beach."

"I still have the Coppertone." I chirped. Dick frowned. He was such a snob when it came to sun tan oil.

We climbed the stairs to Sunland Lodge and entered the rustic lobby. The Karswells were poised on a sofa near the television set. It wasn't turned on, but Jerome Karswell felt some comfort in knowing his face would grace the tiny screen again soon.

We sat on the sofa opposite the Karswells and began our strange tale about his grandfather, the Omega III, the feds, and Cranston Karswell's final disappearance. Jerome still hadn't recovered from the loss of his coffin, especially the martini dispenser part, but he had finally stopped blaming me. He knew the case was far more than a simple coffin heist.

When the conversation slowed, I slipped into one of the lobby phone booths to call Peggy Marshall. I filled her in on the previous night in Chinatown. She was surprised, but not shocked.

"There might be something I can still salvage from this mess," she told me. "I'm working on a novel. I call it *The Case of the Killer's Coffin*. If this isn't a best seller, I'm catching a Greyhound bus back to Grand Rapids."

During brunch in the Mess Hall, Laura Borealis gave a farewell speech, saying she hoped to see us all again next season. We gave her a standing ovation, and the guests began filing out, returning to their cabins to finish packing.

Dick and I decided to take one last walk down to the lake. We watched incoming clouds take on shapes of strange creatures. I sensed the weather was about to change. Tomorrow would be Labor Day, the official end of summer. From here on, it would be indoor nudism for me.

Up on the hill, each cabin was buzzing with naked people stowing luggage into their cars. Dick helped me load my luggage into the Rambler. Li Po's cage squeezed into the back seat. She feasted on vending machine nuts while we packed.

"I promised dad I'd get to the office early today, and I've been stalling," Dick said apologetically. "Things always get backed up when I'm on vacation. I'll have a lot of catching up to do."

"And I have a long drive ahead of me," I said." This time I won't stop at the Twin Car Diner in Solvang; too many bad memories there. I think I'll stop at Pea Soup Andersen's this time."

I'd only known Dick two weeks and yet it felt like I had known him two years. In our separate cars, we joined the long line of vacationers leaving Sunland. Dick followed my car down the mountain road until we reached the 210 Highway. We waved and then split up. He went south, I headed north.

I reached the 101 at Ventura, and 30 minutes later took a break in Santa Barbara, where I parked under the slender palm trees on East Beach. Li Po cracked sunflower seeds in the back seat. At San Luis Obispo, I veered off the 101 to Morro Bay and from there took Highway One through Big Sur. From there, I continued up the coast to San Francisco. When I saw the Cliff House up ahead, I felt like I was home.

Next day, the office looked exactly like I'd left it two weeks ago. The pile of mail on the floor told me Alex had not been here since I went on vacation. I arranged Li Po's cage next to the window that looked out on Chinatown. She seemed pleased, having moved from one Chinatown to another.

My office clothes itched and my girdle stifled me, but I had to get used to it.

Did that bird just say something in Chinese?

As I worked my way through the stack of unpaid bills, Alex limped through the door with the help of a cane. I looked up from my work as he hobbled in.

"Not to worry, Moon Cakes," he cheered. "I won't need this cane for more than a couple months."

Then he spied Li Po.

"What's THAT?"

"That's Li Po," I droned. "our new mascot. Her owner disappeared and her caretaker was kidnapped. She had no one to keep her."

Li Po squawked, "*Gung hay fah choy!*"

"Does that bird speak Chinese? I should have known. How was the vacation?"

"It was fantastic, what there was of it. The case took up too much of my time, but I still had fun. Here's Karswell's check. It should cover your hospital bills and then some. Yes, I loved the camp. In fact, I'm planning to go next year. On the way home I got a tip from a waitress in Santa Cruz about a nude beach at San Gregorio, just south of Pacifica. I think I'll check it out next weekend if it's sunny."

"I see. I take it you're a diehard nudist now."

"You should come, too, Alex. You don't know what you've been missing. It's great!"

"Not on your life! First it's nudism, and the next thing I know I'll be eating lentils and brown rice. No thanks!"

"It'd be better than the cigarettes and Old Ripper you normally have for dinner."

Alex sighed. "I'm not worried," he said. "This is just a phase. Pretty soon you'll forget all about nudism. You'll be collecting postage stamps or volunteering at a parrot rescue farm. You'll see."

I didn't hear him. His words rose into the stale office air and drifted out the window onto the busy street below. I was thinking about Dick's magical hands and our tanning oil sessions back at Sunland.

I just grinned.

»»» *Introducing* «««
THE AUTHOR

Richard Toronto is an American-born writer and science-fiction historian best known for his detailed chronicling of the controversial "Shaver Mystery" and its central figures, Richard S. Shaver and Raymond A. Palmer.

Born in Sonoma, California, Toronto earned a BA in Journalism from CSU Sacramento. He taught film photography to patients at Napa State Hospital for the Criminally Insane. He was a newspaper reporter for a small Bay Area daily, and founded Shavertron—"Your Only Source of Post-Deluge Shaverania"—publishing 29 issues, the longest run of any Shaver Mystery-related fanzine.

Toronto's work is rooted in pulp-era science fiction history and the preservation of esoteric literary subcultures. His narrative blends biography, cultural criticism, and archival research. He began documenting the legacy of fringe sci-fi long before such sub-genres became academically studied.

His detective fiction reflects this pulp era fascination. His debut novel, *Hollywood and Vain*, introduced Alexander "Buster" Blade, a former silent movie child actor turned private detective in postwar San Francisco. The city itself plays a vivid role, blending postwar noir atmosphere tinged with Hollywood McCarthyism.

The series explores post-WWII social dynamics, race, and the emerging detective-fiction tropes in early 20th century California. His bi-racial character, Paloma Liu Tsong, flees small town agricultural life in the Sacramento Delta to become an exotic dancer in the Chinatown club scene. She goes to work for Blade's agency and eventually becomes a private eye in her own novel, *Nudist Camp Confidential.*

Sequels became more genre-bending as the series evolved. *Half Past Satan*, a fast-paced atmospheric novella that takes place in West Marin County, pulls the reader into occult noir and a world where Nazi technology collides with Ouija boards. It merges hard-boiled detective pulp with weird sci-fi/ fantasy, full of 1940s noir slang, tongue-in-cheek humor, and escalating weirdness. The novel is classic mid-century detective fiction with a retro-fantasy twist, exploring philosophical ideas around cults, mysticism, and psychological manipulation. A Goodreads reviewer described *Half Past Satan* as "a sci-fantasy disguised as a detective yarn."

Toronto's books can be found on Amazon.

www.friscodetective.com

www.shavertron.com

httpswww.facebook.com/friscodetective/

https://www.facebook.com/ShavertronPress/

Before You Go:

It is always appreciated when readers leave reviews for our books on Amazon.com. It's the only way a book gets noticed, for ranking on Amazon. Thanks in advance for the review, be it good, bad, or somewhere in the middle.

Marvin D. Fox
Chief, Cook, Bottle Washer,
Atomic Crime Library